PIECES

of the

JOURNEY

PIECES

of the

JOURNEY

A Lifetime of stories and essays

WILBUR L. PIKE III

PIECES OF THE JOURNEY
A Lifetime of stories and essays

iUniverse books may be ordered through booksellers or by contacting:

iUniverse
1663 Liberty Drive
Bloomington, IN 47403
www.iuniverse.com
1-800-Authors (1-800-288-4677)

ISBN: 978-1-4917-7808-1 (sc)
ISBN: 978-1-4917-7807-4 (e)

Library of Congress Control Number: 2015915306

Print information available on the last page.

iUniverse rev. date: 10/15/2015

Contents

Defining Moments

To Dr. John J. Scherer, you have helped me
discover that my core is a worthy one.
I send this to you—and to all of you—from my core to yours.

EMBERS

He blew on the embers of my soul,
and the heat rose within me.
That he knew they were there while I
did not was a surprise and a joy.
But the increasing heat from the embers in my
soul made me sweat and a little afraid.
What if there was more to me than I knew?
What if my con game was up?
What if all the faith I had in humanity was
appropriate and not a shell game?
What if my smug, cynical assurance was really
smug, cynical delusion? What then?
He knew that I was living a lie, and he had never even met me.
If it was obvious to him, could others see it too?
This was deeply perplexing and seductively exciting.
I did not know that there were any embers left in
my soul. I believed that they had been extinguished
by the evil in the world in which I lived.
But he blew, and they ignited.
Now I know they cannot be extinguished—and
that no amount of evil can put them out.
Now I know they are mine to nourish,
and they will sustain me.
I have so much more to learn about that nourishment,
but the journey has begun—started that night
when he blew on the embers of my soul.

INTRODUCTION

For any of those poor souls who've had to sit through any of the countless seminars and workshops I have delivered in my thirty-five-plus years as a management trainer, the concept of this book is easy to grasp. Regardless of the subject matter, I illustrate theory and concepts with anecdotes. I love to tell stories and rely heavily on the oral tradition, a process I've studied a bit.

For many of the peoples on our planet for whom the written word is not the primary medium through which their societies are documented, the oral tradition is far more than a mere means of entertainment. I believe that a well-told story is the ultimate teaching tool. To be able to paint word pictures that the listener can fill and color to satisfy his or her own tastes seems to be an ideal system for customizing the lessons of a story to the needs of each individual.

Fortunately for me, I have always learned new information more quickly and completely whenever I have tried to repackage it to tell others about it. In other words, I view most information coming to me as something I'll need to pass on. I constantly search for better ways to present ideas and information. My father once told me, after my horrible experience as a high school teacher, that no matter what I did for a living, I'd always be a teacher. At the time, I thought he was nuts, but those words have stayed with me—and I cannot deny their truth. When you add that to a remark a fellow YMCA director made, half in jest, half seriously, that I can come up with a story about any subject instantly, you have the premise for this book.

This is a book about the lessons of my life so far. Lessons I've learned about teaching, about management science, about psychology, about relationships, about life. Some of these lessons came to me in countless episodes in my work life: some easy, some hard.

Some came from the social realm. As I look at the stories presented here, most have a measure of pain associated with them, and it was the pain that brought to my attention that something was going on that might be significant. Not all of them were painful however; a few are so happily powerful that I can feel good all over again just telling them to you.

Sam Clemens said of his autobiography that all the information in it was true or ought to be, and that's how I feel about these stories of mine. Their value is designed to be in the messages they carry rather than in the absolute accuracy of their details. I tell them as I remember them. No doubt I have altered the facts to enhance the impact of the lesson, but I have not distorted the facts to the point of manipulation or dishonesty. I have only accurately named some people whose behavior is attractive. The villains have all been cloaked. Sometimes heroes will also remain nameless to protect their privacy.

These stories have been accumulated over a lifetime, so chronology within them may not always be sequential. Some were written more than thirty years ago but read as though they were written yesterday. It is not my intent to be confusing about chronology; it is to retain what I was feeling at the time of writing the pieces.

I have tried to organize these stories by the situations that inspired them. There is a section on lessons from my profession as a management trainer, stories from my association with Camp Mohawk, and a section from my forty years of fishing and traveling with Roger and Jack. There are many stories about my own development and the lessons I've extracted from simply living my life. There are other stories that exist on their own without categorization. Every one of them taught me something important, but I do not expect all of them to do that for you. I do hope that some of them illuminate the hallways of your mind and take you wherever you need them to.

LAUGHING AT LIFE

ARMY

Like many Americans, I have been fascinated lately with the media hype around the imminent danger of paramilitary groups who spend every available minute running around in military garb and conducting war maneuvers in the woods. That picture fascinates me. I have been there, and I know from exhaustive research—I asked at least five of my male friends and my son— that lots of guys have experienced the exhilarating excitement of playing "Army" in the woods. I suppose there is a significant difference among all the people I asked about it and the ones comprising the recently illuminated paramilitary groups, in that each person in my group fondly remembered those games. We all thought it might be fun to do it again, but all of us admitted that we were into the games somewhere between the ages of ten and fourteen—and none of us played the games to prepare ourselves against a certain attack from our own government.

No, we were fighting to keep America safe from foreign enemies. My knowledge of evil foreigners with horribly derisive names often predated our ethnic geography lessons in school. I remember a certain gentle surprise when these peoples were finally introduced to us in class: they were actually real people instead the imaginary monsters we fought so diligently in our forest forts and foxholes. Clearly we were the sociological result of postwar America.

My first real influence in Army games was Neil. He had an imagination as deep as an ocean and the salesmanship necessary to make it all sound real. In addition, he had a great collection of military hats that never ceased to amaze me. We played with anyone we could find in the woods behind his house, and our games were elaborate, complex, and totally captivating. Neil had a grandmother who often suggested really neat ideas to keep us from getting in trouble when we returned home, usually later than we were supposed to. It was she who suggested that we could find a dry place in the woods to keep a change of clothes so that our campfire smoke would not return home with us and give lie to our assurance to our parents that we never made campfires. Our poor parents believed they had frightened us into accepting that as a rule.

Our biggest problem in terms of trouble at home was wet sneakers. There was a wonderful small stream in our woods where one could almost always be certain of an ambush because it could not be crossed without leaving your cover. So whenever you began to carefully step from rock to log to rock, it was more or less an accepted fact that the enemy would open fire and you'd have to run to be able to insist that he'd missed you. It was a much more convincing argument if you were moving. It was also much easier to get your feet wet, and this violation of parental rules was often serious enough to prevent your availability from tomorrow's games. After a while, the situation became so problematic that we were forced to declare the brook as a DMZ; no ambushes were allowed. If you did get caught in one and were shot a little, you could declare yourself not dead.

Even though Neil and I were neighbors, since we didn't go to the same grammar school, he never met Steve. When we reported for the first day of fourth grade, there was a new kid. He wasn't very big and had a big, happy, round face. Even cooler, though, was that fact that he had a seriously southern accent. He was from North Carolina and sounded it. We were captivated almost immediately. Looking back now through the analytical lens of a psychologist, I realize that Steven Metcalf was probably the strongest natural leader I'd ever met to that point in my life. To a group of nine-year-old boys who wished that the school would burn down and take all the teachers with it, a strong, natural leader among our age group was a profoundly powerful influence.

It did not take us long to realize that Steve was seriously into military lore and far more advanced in his development of it than we were. The combination of his knowledge of Army, our desire to know more about it, and his infectious leadership skills resulted in an "Army Club" that met at Steve's house after school and on Saturdays. We had a full platoon with a pecking order of ranks, attainable through tests and Steve's whim, and designated separate sections of his basement for enlisted men and officers. He knew that we would not stay motivated as perpetual enlisted men, so the roster of the other officers (he was always a colonel) was a rather fluid list.

We played that way throughout the winter of our first year together, with occasional forays out into his backyard but not with any serious maneuvers into the woods. When spring finally came, Steve announced our first big bivouac into the woods in and around Charcoal Pond. The excitement built for the weeks before the big event, and the weather cooperated perfectly on the designated day.

Rather than the highly imaginary games I had been exposed to with my old friend Neil, this was different. We met as ordered at the dam. Steve arrived in full field garb with several cases and packs we were unfamiliar with. He had a replica World War II rifle and a real combat helmet. He issued colored armbands to clearly designate two teams and several maps of the area he had drawn. There was a specific target (a flag) hidden in a tree clearly shown on the map. He also stated clearly what the rules were for getting shot and presented a series of graduated outcomes—depending on how seriously you were shot—that ranged from being out of commission for ten minutes for a questionable "wing shot" all the way to totally decommissioned and reduced to observer for a clear "kill shot." I remember a certain feeling of exciting fear that I might not be up to the tasks set for me in Steve's plan for the daylong event, but I was totally committed to trying to do my best. I also knew that the day would be unlike any previous experience with Army.

As I look back all these years later, I am astounded by the organizational and leadership skills that Steve Metcalf demonstrated. I have only seldom seen them in others in my life and am staggered at the thought that on that Saturday at Charcoal Pond, they were the apparent natural product of a ten-year-old boy.

As luck would have it, I was assigned to Steve's platoon. I was thrilled. Since he knew where the target was and the others didn't, he gave them a five-minute lead. As we began to move out, he cautioned us repeatedly that they had probably assigned snipers to fire on us as we followed. It only took a few minutes for me to realize that I was traveling with a true commando master. In no time, he had camouflaged his uniform and encouraged us to do the same. He never walked on paths; he would check out the next area, figure out where the snipers would most likely be, and then move into the thickest woods to sneak up behind them. In the first half hour, we had found and "destroyed" nearly all their snipers. He was absolutely awesome, and we all began to emulate his behavior with a great deal of confident bravado.

When we reached the stream that separated us from our target, we whispered hoarsely about how and where they would be expecting us to cross the stream. After careful consultation, he decided on the safest place to cross; in true leadership style, he insisted on being the first man over. The spot he chose was an unlikely one (and therefore thought of as safer) that required Steve to get a running start before leaping across to the middle of the stream to a rock and bounding the rest of the way across. It was a bold plan.

We spread out near our edge of the stream to provide cover fire should he need it. His run and jump were so truly beautiful to behold that we were much more interested in watching him than we were in scanning the other side for snipers. As he landed in complete control, rifle at the ready on the rock in the middle of the stream, Ronnie Evans, the opposing force leader, calmly stepped from behind a tree on the other side of the brook and fired once at our leader in what was clearly an undeniable "kill shot." We were flabbergasted. We had come to believe that Steve Metcalf was infallible and immortal. Ronnie did the deed with such aplomb and arrogance. We were so shocked that we never even thought to return fire, and Ronnie proceeded to wound several of our group before we got our wits about us.

But the real picture in my mind of this momentous event was what happened next. Steve had given us all strict instructions before teams were set that he'd tolerate no petty arguments about whether or not you were really shot. No arguments about "you missed me" or "your gun wasn't loaded.'" If you get shot, admit it and learn from the experience. Now as Ronnie's imaginary bullet sank deep into Steve's body, he shuddered, rose to his full height, spun to look back with incredulousness and disappointment at those assigned to protect him, and fell erect, facedown into the stream with a massive splash. As I looked at him with my mind-set of wet feet meant punishment, we watched as his "dead body" floated facedown and fully dressed past us for what seemed like a long, long time. Man, did Steve Metcalf know how to play Army.

He had chosen a point for this bit of theater where the stream curved, and he simply floated around the bend and out of sight. For a long time, none of us could move. Even Ronnie stood out in the clear, and we did not shoot at each other. We weren't sure whether we were actors in this play or audience, but one thing was clear: this guy was motivated by a much higher level of commitment than we were. It was clear that we were in the presence of a master, and we were collectively mired in serious awe.

Finally somebody broke the spell with a halfhearted shot at Ronnie who promptly disappeared back behind his tree.

For a long time, there was an oppressive silence. Our next-in-command, Vinnie, ordered us to move out downstream to find Steve and make sure he was "properly buried." We all followed eagerly. When we finally bushwhacked our way around the bend in the river, Steve was gone. He had simply disappeared. This was extremely upsetting to us all, and we began to call loudly for him without any thoughts about revealing our position to the enemy. They, however, regrouped on the other side of the stream, crossed at the point we'd just left, and calmly captured our entire force by surrounding us. It was intensely sad and very embarrassing.

I hated Ronnie for being the cold-blooded killer that he was, and all the fun of Army was gone for me as we were marched back to the dam to end the game. Our leader was dead and missing, and we had let him down and lost the game. We marched fifty yards or so when we heard the familiar verbalizations of Steve Metcalf's rifle. Several of the front guard of our captors went down, and some of us had the presence of mind to take their weapons and open up on the rest. In short order, we had the upper hand. We took the flag from them, which they had already retrieved, and regrouped with our leader.

Naturally, Ronnie arose from his "killed" position and vehemently protested Steve's apparent reincarnation. Steve did not defend himself until Ronnie ran out of breath, and then he ceremoniously revealed the metal map case he had been wearing across his chest. It had a clear bullet hole in the front—but not the back. He opened it, reached inside, removed a rifle slug, and tossed it to Ronnie.

"Saved my life," he said. "The shock knocked me out for a couple of minutes, but I guess the cold water snapped me out of it. You should have gone for my legs first, Ronnie, and then finished me off once I was down."

What joy! What sweet revenge! What a guy! We were snapped out of our victorious celebration by the cold, angry voice of our leader. He announced that although we had gotten lucky enough to win this battle, it was due with no thanks to us. He suggested that our training from then on was not going to be much fun and that generally he was extremely disappointed in us. Such talk was like an arrow through my heart, and I felt lower than I did when I thought he was dead. I eagerly accepted his criticism and swore to myself that I would pay much more attention during our next training sessions so that I would never be unreliable again.

So don't try to scare me, all you paramilitary idiots. I am not afraid of you or of the government either. I was trained in the classroom and the field by Colonel Steve Metcalf, so you had better not mess with me. My only worry is that I have not heard from—or of—Steve Metcalf since 1960, and if he's still alive and leading any of those groups, then we should all be afraid, very afraid.

FATHER HANOVER

I spent most of my childhood as a forced practitioner of Roman Catholicism. In fact, I know very few people who, as young Catholics, spent their childhoods in any other way. My plight was perhaps worsened by the fact that I went to public school. My father was a Congregationalist, and he had to agree not to "interfere" in the spiritual development of his children in order to get married in a Catholic church in the first place. He was also a public grammar-school custodian, and my mother taught in the same school. I went to the school where my parents both worked. I liked it there. I attended school with lots of people who were different than me. They came from all walks of life, representing the full socioeconomic spectrum of Bridgeport, Connecticut, in the mid-1950s.

My mother enrolled me in catechism classes for several years. To me, this was primarily a form of punishment. Since the content of most of those classes included threats of all sorts of horrible afterlife outcomes, I was never dissuaded from the perception that Catholicism was synonymous with pain, fear, and punishment. I still am perplexed by the idea that—in order to show us how much he loved us—God arranged for the horrible and unnatural death of his only son. The classes were either after school or on Saturday mornings. It is simply a fact of the human condition that any normal little boy would have to be forced to sit in religious school during those hours. There were perhaps a thousand other things more attractive to him after school or on Saturday mornings.

The nuns who got the unlucky draw of having to teach the public-school kids often did not embrace the assignment. We were to them the great unwashed, and they certainly didn't want to wash us. The whole experience for me was one of resistance, threats, and worry. The worry came as a result of trying to believe the content of the training while facing the challenges of life. I was told, for example, that to attend worship in a Protestant church was to ensure eternal damnation. I was also told to love and respect my parents, which I didn't need to be told to do. Every other week, when my father took me to the Congregational church, I thought I was choosing between my father and my own salvation, which was pretty heavy stuff for a young boy to consider.

Later, when I went through the gauntlet of confirmation classes as an adolescent, I began to argue a bit with the nuns who taught me. The good ones (and there were several good ones) used that repartee as an opportunity for learning. The others came down hard and heavy. The final blow to any respect for the theology at all came when the Church refused to recognize my name. There is no Saint Wilbur, you see. How about the middle name, Luther? Oh my, no. The church records, if they still exist, will show my confirmation as John Pike. This was the last straw of insult to a young adolescent, for whom the development of a personal identity is a major big deal.

My mother, sister, and I went to Mass every Sunday until I was sixteen. Then I told her I would drive myself, and I did—to anywhere else but Mass. Up until then, I became the weekly target of Father Hanover. I know that I was not actually his target. It just felt like it then. He was a disagreeable, ruddy-faced Irishman with a nasty self-righteous disposition. He would visit our weekly religious school classes and growl his dissatisfaction that our parents were not following the teachings of the Church and sending us to his school as full-time (tuition-paying) students. I hated him for treating me like a second-class citizen and for suggesting that my parents were evil, wrong, or misguided.

Father Hanover's real stage was the altar. From there, nearly every Sunday, he railed on and on about the deterioration of the fabric of society in Bridgeport, which he felt was due to the lack of discipline in the public schools. I would sit stiffly next to my mother, whose professionalism was being insulted, and bristle as he complained about the public high school kids racing up and down the street in front of the rectory. Of course, my next-door neighbor, Billy, a product of parochial schools since kindergarten, was the wildest kid I knew behind the wheel. Father Hanover sung this theme week after week, and I couldn't wait until I could find a way to escape.

I knew that I was given a short two-week reprieve every summer when I went away to camp. Ah, camp. That sweet time in the year when I could be on my own, spending my days learning by doing the coolest things in life. I lived the entire year to go to camp. No matter when it was during the year, I always knew the exact number of days until I could go again. And to add to the pure sweetness of it all was the reality of no Father Hanover harangues on Sunday morning.

Such was my state of mind when I was perhaps fourteen years old and joyfully arrived at camp. As a senior camper, I was in an elite social and skill group, having passed all the basic training classes in canoeing, swimming, wood crafts, and horseback riding in previous years. No beginner classes for us, no sirree. We were the advanced group. Life was wonderful.

I tried to get out of having to ride the bus into town on Sunday to go to Mass, but once your records showed "Catholic," you were pretty much locked into going. It wasn't that a YMCA camp in those days was so interested in the proper religious training of their non-Protestant clientele. It was because they were glad to have the paid campers in camp and did not want to risk appearing rigid about whom they'd accept. So on Sundays during camp, we Catholics were roused before reveille and loaded on a bus before breakfast and taken to town to Mass. Mostly we hated it. The counselors who took us were the only Catholic members of the staff; naturally, they hated it too.

That year, I took a more positive attitude. While it was certainly no fun to have to interrupt the happiness of normal camp life with a trip to Mass, at least it might be interesting to experience a different church. Maybe there'd be a nice priest. Since I had recently completed my confirmation, I was at least mildly curious to see how it was in a different church. I didn't even remember going to Mass in the years previous to that one, but I know I did. Apparently I had just zoned out until it was over. But that year was different. I had become intellectually curious and was beginning to really compare the teachings of Mother Church to other ideas I had heard about. And more than anything, I wanted to see what the Church could be like without Father Hanover in it to berate me and my family for merely existing.

I found out that we were going to a different church than we had in other years. I was excited about that, given that I had to go at all. I liked the church as soon as I saw it.

First of all, it had lots of sunlight, which was a new idea for me. All my previous experiences were in churches that seemed content to treat sunlight like temptation to be avoided. Not only was it sunny inside this one, but there was a youth choir singing. This was really cool. I realize now that the Church might have hooked me early in life if they'd tried to use music to do it. By the time Mass was beginning, I was really enjoying myself—maybe for the first time—in the process of worship.

The nightmare that followed has stayed with me all these years and pushes me to write this story now. For now, sunlight blazing in, choir belting out a tune, out onto the altar walked the altar boys—and Father Hanover! Clouds blocked the sun as he looked up at the choir and frowned. They stopped singing. There was no escape, and my spirit took a direct hit between the eyes that went straight to my heart. The shock was devastating. When I saw his face, I realized that he so hated me for being a public-school kid that he found me at camp and had arranged to follow me there. The power of his evil was overwhelming. I was powerless to protect myself from his reach. I was like a plant that finally produced a bud, only to be ground into the earth by his boot heel.

I do not remember the rest of that Mass, the ride back to camp, or anything at all about going to Mass from camp anywhere after that day. As I said, as soon as I got my driver's license, I stopped going to Mass forever. Several years later, I met a guy in high school whose family was very close to the Church. In fact, Father Hanover dined regularly at their house. He was the one who told me that Father Hanover had a twin brother who was a priest too, but it was too late. The damage was done and beyond repair.

Perhaps the only positive from this entire experience was that it caused me to doubt. I began to study a bit about other religions, perhaps to appease my guilt for rejecting Catholicism. I realized that there were a bunch of organized religions in the world—and that the majority of the population of the planet is not Catholic or even Christian. I also found out that most of those organized religions shouted loudly that theirs was the one, true answer. It didn't take me long to feel that if more than two thousand different religions each had different answers to the same questions, the odds were that none of them had it totally right. I learned that spirituality is a mental state and can be learned and developed. I learned that being devout wasn't all about memorizing rules and history. It was more about making your spiritual beliefs the force you lived your life by. I found out, for example, that Native Americans were far more devout than the people who defeated them.

If Father Hanover had realized those things, this story would not exist—and it wouldn't need to. He taught me to resist intolerance, but I don't think he meant to.

COSMICALLY ALIGNED MISERY

There are times in everyone's life when a series of otherwise unrelated events become related events at the worst possible moment, in the worst possible way. These are those moments when you alone can truly understand the interplay of the factors that have cosmically coincided to bring you a kind a serendipitous misery that is virtually impossible to explain to anyone else. Even if you try to explain, the receiver often begins to look at you in an odd, slightly detached way that causes him or her to subtly move away from you. Of course, if you have any sense of reality, you realize that—based on what you are explaining—moving away from you is a completely understandable behavior.

So get ready to perhaps move away from me because I am about to try to relate a single event, which all by itself isn't much of a story. But when viewed from my vantage point, it comprises an experience of situational complexity that still remains within my memory as a clear and powerful image.

Let's start with the garden. It was spring, and I was prepping for the garden planting. I had finally broken down and arranged to have a truckload of new topsoil delivered to replenish the tired soil of my garden. I bought the garden along with the house. It is a big one—perhaps thirty feet by sixty feet—fenced, and very well cared for by the previous owners. In fact, since they were both retired, it had been their pride and joy. It was also more than fifty yards away from my house.

When Frankie came with the small dump truck of topsoil, he needed to do some pretty fancy backing up across the lawn, around trees and stone walls, all under the watchful eye of my (former) wife who was very focused on him not ruining the lawn. The task would have been daunting even for Frankie, who was a professional truck driver, on firm, dry terrain. But he did not have that luxury for this event. It had been raining for days, the soaking continuous rains of spring. The old garden was mostly mud, and virtually all the lawn was spongy at best and submerged in several spots.

I was surprised when Frankie showed up with my dirt. It was raining again that day, and he said it would be the only chance he would have for the delivery. We walked the pathway I had planned for him to get the soil over to the garden, and he kept looking at me like I was delusional, which apparently I was. He backed up the slight hill from the driveway to the back lawn and promptly got stuck. He rolled back down and tried again in a different spot with the same result, not to mention a second set of deep tire tracks in the grass. In an effort to prevent noise from my wife about the lawn, I told him to dump the load there. I would move it to the garden by wheelbarrow. So that's how the big pile of topsoil ended up directly behind the house. Every time I (or my wife) came or went out the side door of the house, we looked at that anomaly on our lawn.

It was June, and I was trying to arrange my life to be certain that I could attend the fishing week with the boys. We were heading for Cape Cod that year, which would be a new and exciting venture for us. From my wife's perspective, it didn't matter where we were going; she was against it. In fact, she had been against every other fishing trip I had ever been on, and no amount of discussion or negotiation had weakened or dissipated her efforts to thwart the trip.

I had made pretty good progress on the topsoil pile by that time. In fact, I had moved maybe three-quarters of it. It was still often raining, and by then, the remaining pile was mostly mud.

Let's suspend these events for a moment and focus instead on my job. I am an independent organizational psychologist with my own consulting practice. It had taken several years to build my practice to the successful level I was maintaining at the time of this story. One of the perks I had allowed myself from those rewards was the purchase of a Peugeot 505 Turbo sedan. It was two years old when I bought it, but I loved that car like no other I have owned before or since. It was a rocket, comfortable beyond description, and my pride and joy. It had all the bells and whistles: heated seats, special road lamps, and electric everything, including a sunroof that I especially loved.

To make the fight about going on the fishing trip worse, my largest and most profitable client scheduled a breakfast meeting for the Tuesday of the week of the trip. I could not convince him to move the meeting, so I told my buddies that I would come to the Cape separately, leaving immediately after my breakfast meeting at nine thirty on Tuesday. They left on Saturday and would have more than two days of fishing before I got there. This was a huge concession on my part, but I could not see any other way short of risking my best client.

In one last-ditch effort to find any kind of common negotiation position with my wife, I agreed to complete the topsoil transfer before I left. When I agreed to that task, I had four days in which to get the job done. Normally, it would have been easy.

Then it rained. It didn't just rain; it motivated a desire to find plans for an ark. I lost three of those four possible workdays. Finally it cleared a bit on Monday, and I got much of the remaining pile moved before the skies opened again and drove me indoors. Since I had maybe two hours of labor remaining, I set my alarm for Tuesday morning at five thirty.

When I went out, it was still pouring, as it had all night. I was miserably shoveling mud as fast as conditions would allow, soaked to the skin, but I was determined to complete the task, keep my word, make my meeting on time, and finally break away to a few of days of chasing stripers and bluefish. I had already resolved myself to the ugliness of this reality, but I had found the silver lining I needed for motivation: the solo drive in my rocket to the Cape, loaded with my rods and other gear. It was my one truly happy thought in the midst of the misery of backbreaking shoveling and pushing the loaded wheelbarrow through lakes of standing water to the garden and repeating the whole process, soaking wet. It went slower than I had anticipated, and I began to hurry, adding a touch of panic to the situation. I had more or less convinced myself that I could not be more miserable.

As the heavy rain continued, my mood deteriorating with each shovelful, my son stopped out on the porch on his way to high school. He knew the whole story, and it would be another story to explain why I did not get any help from this strong young man, but suffice it to say that he was enjoying my situation immensely.

He stopped on the porch and said, "Hi ya, Pop! Looks a little wet out there. How's it going?" He knew how it was going, how I got to that point, and what misery really looked like. He made small talk for five or ten minutes; the topic was how muddy the dirt was.

I contemplated going after him with the shovel, but I didn't think I had the time.

He said, "Well, I gotta go catch my bus. There is one other thing I think you ought to know." He grinned widely. "Your sunroof is wide open and has been all night. Have a good time at the Cape." Off he skipped, laughing, down the driveway.

In my heart, I don't think have forgiven him for that glee— even all these years later. In any case, I raced to the car. When I opened the driver's door, water actually flowed out from the floor. I ran and got my keys, wondering what would happen to the car electrically when I turned on the ignition. Fortunately, nothing bad did happen—and I was able to close the roof. When I settled into that wonderfully padded foam driver's seat, water gushed out from every seam. Even though I was already soaked to the skin, that gushing water made me feel even wetter.

I returned to my shoveling job and completed it through the adrenaline from my pure rage. Before my meeting, I spent as much time as I had sponging the water out of the car. I drove to my meeting on top of a poncho and wore my rain suit. Every move in the car caused new sources of water to flow. Somehow the electrical system was not compromised.

On my drive to the Cape, still sitting on that poncho, I stopped every now and then to mop up newly released water. I don't remember too much about the fishing on that trip, but I do remember the culmination of otherwise unrelated events, facts, conditions, and emotions that resulted in perhaps the greatest several hours of misery I ever experienced. So far, anyway.

DISCOVERIES

THE DESTINATION RUSE

The concept of an actual destination for a person's quest in life is a fabricated delusion. It isn't a bad or evil delusion—and perhaps it is even necessary to help us maintain direction or prevent madness—but the idea that we have a "place" to arrive at or a target to say we hit is a game we play with ourselves.

For those of us who strive for personal achievement, or in my case, teach others to do it as well, we must have a target to aim at. We focus on that target, create detailed plans based on what we know about the target, and use the target to keep our sails filled and our compass directions relevant. We become so focused on the target that we forget that we made it all up. It was just a contrivance to make sure that the journey was meaningful. We just aren't satisfied enough with the quest itself for its own sake. Merely playing in the game isn't enough. We need to find a way to manufacture a win out of the whole deal.

While the destination ruse drives nearly all our behavior, it is never fully satisfying or rewarding because it isn't really what the game is all about. I used to think that the only real destination, in terms of a truly final outcome, was death. But since I have now experienced the loss of some of those closest to me, I don't think that anymore. The power of the presence of those who have reached what society says is the final destination in my life is real and undeniable. I believe they are still traveling as am I. Our forms may have changed, but that's really all that is different.

I can easily contend that our current concept of death is a created ruse as well. In fact, it is the best we can do to have an ultimate destination. Religions have latched onto the idea that there is more to travel after death, and that becomes a really compelling attraction for us. But even their models of what follows death are new destinations, final achievements, and places where we need to journey no more. I don't believe it.

For those of us who want our lives to count for something, consider what we do as soon as we reach important destinations. We create the next ones. Oh sure, we may bask for a while in the achievement of arriving where we aimed, but while we are sitting in that satisfied place, we are hatching new plans because that is simply what we do. We're hardwired to do it, and we do not know how to understand life without it.

Trying to understand life without the measuring stick of destination achievement is my new created destination. The richness and value in life is all about the journey itself; the destination is not the goal. To keep on keepin' on is what it is all about, and the true lessons that we need to discover are all hidden in the journey, not at the destination, because the destination isn't real.

Charlie, Me and Selective Excellence

I have a good friend named Charlie. We've been friends for more than thirty-five years, although a few years back—for lots of questionable reasons—we drifted apart. I think a distinguishing characteristic of the full concept of "good friends" is that despite a lack of contact or proximity, you always think of each other as good friends.

I have rejoined the frequent company of my friend Charlie and couldn't be happier. I love the guy as a man. We have jillions of things in common. We both love the water, quiet time with nature, a good story, a clever joke, and most powerfully, the joy of music. As I say, as a man, I love Charlie, and as a fellow musician, I stand aside in complete awe at his genius. Quite simply, he is the most gifted sax player and overall musician I have heard anywhere, anytime. Period.

Years ago, when Charlie and I were arguing about something, certainly insignificant, the discussion of the topic lasted over several weeks. We'd yell at each other, threaten each other, resort to all sorts of creative obscene name-calling, and know that throughout the delightful process, our friendship was never in jeopardy. As he has done many times since, Charlie said something so simple and profound that it took me weeks to really understand it. When I did, I found that I knew myself a lot better. He said, "I've never known a man harder to be friends with. It takes a lot of energy, but the payoff almost always exceeds the effort."

I was not as interested in the complimentary part of that message as I was about the hard to be friends with part. I knew instantly that he was right, and it took me a long time to really understand the why of it all. The point is that he could capture the essence of our relationship in so few words and that I understood him intuitively and completely.

In any case, I am reminded of that comment because reconnecting with Charlie has had an equally profound effect on me again. This time, I can learn about myself because I can so easily see how he's grown up in the years since we parted. I'm not talking about the traditional concept of growing up. I'm talking about growing up inside the one thing he does better than everybody else.

When Charlie and I played together (he the virtuoso, me the journeyman) he had a well-deserved reputation for extreme nervousness before and during performances. Everybody who played with him knew about it because it never made logical sense for him to be nervous about performance when his level of ability was so much higher than the rest of us.

Well, that's all gone now. He's simply outgrown it. I went to hear him play this fall for the first time in more than ten years, and naturally his sax work was awesome. We were seated in a crowded lounge, and I could not actually see the band unless I stood up. As I sat listening to a tune I had asked him to play, I was surprised to hear a male vocal solo, which was really excellently performed.

It wasn't until the second phrase that I realized that it was my friend singing, and the joy of that form of expression for him was clearly evident to my ear. Lots of instrumental musicians learn to sing passably well to ensure marketability, me among them, but that's not what I was listening to when Charlie sang. I was listening to the vocal expression of his musical genius, and I was, once again, in awe. It was clear that the audience got it too, but I did not expect them to get it the way I did. The power of our friendship has always been fueled by an intuitive understanding of large complex ideas conveyed in just a few words or with a key phrase. We each know how the other guy thinks; we are powerfully compatible, and in that very hip tenor voice, his song spoke volumes to me.

It spoke about coming of age, of finally accepting that you're really good at a thing, and realizing it's okay to admit it. It sang about the joy of simply being yourself and having the outcome result in a really positive experience for other people, like giving a gift without the loss of any resources. And as always, his words challenged me to look inside myself to see if, when, or where that might have happened to me in the past ten years as it had so clearly happened for Charlie.

I am fascinated with the idea of exceptional performance. I have always been drawn to questions about why one person can learn to do a thing that lots of other people do too, but that one person does it just miles better than everybody else. There's been lots of research about it from a psychological analysis viewpoint, and while I find that research interesting, it doesn't serve me very well when I sit in tears of joy from the sheer beauty of Charlie's work. I think that my quest to understand this phenomenon comes from a need to understand the essence of the human spirit. Compared to the power of exceptional human performance, most other subjects pale a bit.

I wonder if I have settled into some performance area with the same joy my friend has—and I believe I have—although mine doesn't have the romance and glitter of Charlie's or anywhere near the same size of appreciative audience. When I lost my job as a high school teacher more than twenty years ago, my father told me not to give up on who I really was. He said, "You're a teacher. It's in your blood; it's who you are as a person. No one can take it from you, and if you will let it, it will carry you wherever you need to go." Like a dope, I thought he was just expressing his dissatisfaction because I'd lost my job. I thought I'd dismissed his comments as just father advice stuff that I already knew, but that remark has stayed with me for all these years. I have thought about it long, hard, and often. I think I finally get it now.

I am effective in the front of a classroom just as Charlie is effective with his sax. What my audience experiences is the cumulative effect of thirty years of learning, starting with the fact that I have natural (noncognitive) ability to begin with. All my life, if I could talk and get you to even half listen, I could influence your thoughts. Later I realized that if I could also shut up, I could learn how your mind does its thing—and then I could influence you more completely or more easily. Like my friend, I studied and learned to communicate in the styles of others who were acknowledged as good at it. All of that was preparation for the development of my own system of effectiveness.

When we were in our twenties, Charlie told me a story about an old friend. Walter was arguably the best musician Torrington ever produced. Walter was, by the time I met him, a drunk. Charlie's father was his friend and looked after him. When Charlie was a teenager, he learned to copy the tone and style of Paul Desmond and was eager to show Walter that he could sound like Desmond. Walter, in his inimitable style, said something along the lines of, "Big deal. You haven't really done anything until you can sound like yourself and you're as satisfied as you are when you sound like Desmond." While Charlie was seriously deflated at the time, the lesson stayed with him ever since.

And so I have become a teller of stories. I have studied the styles of countless storytellers and have, as does Charlie, a few who still inspire me and to whose level of excellence I aspire. Yet I am happiest when I simply let my own style loose. What results is a combination of fact, embellished fact, fiction, and fantasy that combine to move an audience to a new place. To me, the spoken word can be music, and I know a million tunes. I seldom tell them the same way twice. I have invented people who don't actually exist who have supposedly said memorable things to me, which I can repeat as theirs and not risk appearing arrogant to my audience. I will do nearly anything to help my audience get my message, but my real hope is that it'll only be my message until they get it and then their brains will alter it in some way that is meaningful and impactful for them.

One of the created people I quote is an uncle who loves to retell his favorite stories. He says that events get to be called stories only if they're repeated. He is quoted by me as saying, "If you've heard this before, don't stop me. My guess is that you'll listen to a favorite song or symphony over and over again—so why not this story?" I really like the feeling of that sentiment.

So, play on my friend, as will I. I hope you have learned to descend into the warmth and serenity of being able to do the thing you love well because few others ever have the opportunity. Never take it for granted or let others do that to you. I never will because when you do it and I can hear it, I am nearly as happy as you ought to be.

ME AND SAM

Sam and I went fishing tonight. I've been fishing for years with Roger and Jack, but it's pretty rare that I go fishing with Sam. I was fishing for relaxation and all the other reasons I have fished for most of my life. Sam was fishing to survive. His patience and skill were nothing short of a working miracle. He stands still until the fish don't even know he's standing right there with them. When he has been patient long enough and all the other conditions are favorable, he is presented with a chance to survive, but he must demonstrate even more skill. There must be varying levels of basic skills—even among the other great blue herons—and I believe Sam's skills must be among the top of his species. The fact that he is alive and as large as he is offers irrefutable proof that his survival skills are more than adequate to meet the needs of his life.

Maybe it's wrong to say that Sam fishes for survival and I don't. Maybe I do too—only not with such a direct line between success and survival. It's a good thing that the line isn't too direct because my fishing skills would have resulted in my demise long ago if I had to produce fish to eat. Maybe I fish to survive as an emotional requirement. Maybe I have simply been able to tune in behaviorally to an activity that makes me feel good. It always has, and I hope it always will.

I had the honor of fishing with Sam because I was living on a lovely pond in Connecticut. To live on the water has been a dream of mine for as long as I can remember, but the pathway by which I arrived there was certainly not one I would have imagined during any of those dreams. At age forty-five, I apparently had run full speed into some sort of midlife experience.

I hate the labeling system we use in America to acknowledge the crucial passages of life. When my life upheaval at age forty-five is viewed by people who know me, it seems a simple and complete pronouncement to reduce the whole intensely complex and painful process to an almost offhand remark by saying, "Oh, he's just having a midlife crisis."

It's as though the total disruption of the most profound values in my life with all the accompanying rejections of behaviors for which I have been reliable for twenty-five years could be reduced to something insignificant simply by having something to call it. I realize that I have been guilty of that behavior myself at one time or another in my life, but now I know that doing so caused me to miss valuable opportunities to really understand the passages of our lives.

Closely associated with this reduction of complex human functions through labeling is the equally ridiculous idea that I'll snap out of it, which is much like the experience of returning to this reality from the alternate one of hypnosis. The fact of the matter is that what I have experienced in the past twenty months or so is a culmination of every other moment of my life, and this process is all part of a larger process. I expect to emerge from this passageway and into another, and when I do, I will be a far different person than I was when I entered it. This isn't some temporary aberration that has infected my mind, which, if properly treated, I'll be cured of. This is my life now, and I am living it the best way I know how.

I am immensely impressed by Sam's ability to survive. He doesn't have the need, apparently, for lots of careful analysis about his needs and how to achieve them. He's a heron, and he behaves like one, pure and simple. In many ways, I want to try to return to some of that simplicity, which is the essence of Sam. I am a man and seek to behave like one. That in and of itself has highly complex possibilities with myriad choices for behavior, but I don't need excess levels of introspective analysis to choose correctly. James Thurber wrote an essay titled "Leave Your Mind Alone," and I agree with him fully.

Since I was a boy, I have wanted to be alone on a lake in a canoe. I have become an avid fisherman as a result of that drive because I haven't been very good at sitting somewhere without a productive outcome. Now as I sit there and watch Sam work, I realize that if I simply leave myself alone, I am never idle anyway. I don't need to program myself to find ways to feel satisfied; they'll just happen because that's who I am.

This midlife deal that I'm into is virtually impossible for others close to me to fully grasp, and no wonder. I have suggested in word or deed that everything they have come to rely on me to be is uncertain. I have left my wife of twenty-seven years, reestablished my self-employment, moved into this little house on this pond, and spent lots of time and effort writing. I don't want to worry too much about the world I walked away from. When I am "counseled" by others in my life whom I respect, their primary motive is to help me return safely to the world I've left because they like me when I'm there. In one sense, my rejection of it all seems threatening to each of them, and I can understand that reaction easily. The problems come from the fact that they are far less willing to accept me as I am, whatever it is, and insist that the pathways by which I have been happy before should continue to serve me for the rest of my life. In most cases, the people who send those messages most loudly are the ones who have done that for themselves. They have reached some sort of baseline of satisfaction and seek to maintain it by rejecting anything that threatens it. I understand because I was there with them for many years.

I seek to return to the basic lessons of life, which Sam can teach me. He will consider virtually any behavior if he can see an increased opportunity to survive. He has no internally imposed rules for his life because the external ones are so clear and so positive. His ability to survive is determined solely by his ability to survey the environment, apply what he knows about behavior in a predictive way, and place himself in the right place at the right time often enough to keep his belly full. Sounds like a pretty good plan to me.

I realize that merely keeping my belly full isn't enough to truly sustain me, but all the rest will simply follow because I am a man with a reasonably good brain and a desire to have my life matter in some way. I don't need to worry about the constant scrutinizing of life any more than Sam needs to worry about it. If I leave myself alone, it'll happen because that's who I am.

Thanks for the lesson, Sam. Teach on.

SIMPLE JUSTICE

I suppose one of the more difficult pieces of growing up revolves around dealing with a young boy's realization that the adults in his world aren't always right and that as he grows older, he can see the faults in their logic and behavior. His is a world of more or less simple black and white, right and wrong. Just getting that sorting done clearly is trouble enough without adding shades of gray. By adolescence, some boys can become cynical, sarcastic, and arrogant when faced with the view that much of the adult world is screwed up—and that's the world they are on the threshold of entering.

It is safe to say that I was the epitome of this syndrome by the time I was twelve or thirteen. I was a wise guy whenever I was in a situation in which I was relatively sure of myself, a coward otherwise. I was also the smallest kid in seventh grade and eighth grade—male or female—which did not help much with my fragile self-esteem. I had already been transferred from the grammar school where my parents worked to the one in my neighborhood (where I actually belonged).

I was the new kid in seventh grade, and I soon had my share of being pushed around by the inevitable pecking order of the boys in my class. I was clearly in the bottom group in terms of size and strength, but I wasn't challenged by anyone else in that group because the risk to them was too great. Should they lose in a fight with me, their status would drop dangerously, so mostly there was lots of trash talk but not much else.

I also found out that I was smarter than many of the bigger, older kids in seventh grade. Their presence in the class at all was testimony to their intellectual challenges. For the most part, they left me alone. There is some protection from being able to think and verbalize enough cleverness to prevent getting punched out. All of these dynamics went into the hopper of my development while I waited for the growth spurt that my mother reassured me every day would come.

I really wanted to be an athlete. I was relatively coordinated and could figure out the logic and angles of most games pretty quickly, which helped offset the size limitations that I brought to any game. On the weekends in the fall, we played tackle football at the park on the other side of the school. As it happened, our house was nearly a mile from the school, so I rode my bike about halfway to a friend's house and then walked the rest of the way every day with my pals. When I played football, the distance to the field was maybe a mile and a half, which is a long walk. I walked because I could not carry all my equipment on the bike, and wearing it all was so uncool that I wouldn't even consider it.

For about three weeks in the fall, as I rode home from Jimmy's house after school, about every other day, an obnoxious, yapping little dog ran down from his backyard doghouse, circled once or twice around me and then moved in and bit me on the ankle. After the fifth occurrence of this event, I got the name of the dog's owner from Jimmy.

After about the tenth attack, one that broke the skin and drew blood, I told my father about it. He offered to call the family and tell them about it since he was big on dog discipline. When he called, the woman was rude, loud, and apparently as obnoxious as her dog. She screamed that there was no way I was telling the truth because her dog was always tied up and never left the yard. She said he should worry more about keeping me from lying and less time harassing the neighbors about their dogs.

He hung up the phone and said, "The next time the dog attacks you, defend yourself in any way you can think of." I knew he was furious with this stupid woman, but he did not say so because in our house the lessons about respect for adults were more important than almost anything else, especially for a thirteen-year-old wise guy.

The following weekend, there was a big football game scheduled at the park. Some kids from another school wanted to play us, which was a pretty big deal. I had recently established myself as a guy who could carry the ball and somehow avoid tackles (fear is a great motivator), and I was eager to play and maybe continue my slow progress up the pecking order.

The game was a massacre. The giants were from a high school. I got pummeled in every way possible until the game was thankfully over. After our annihilation was complete, I walked back to Jimmy's house to rest before the long walk home. Tired, beaten, and depressed, I began the trek home and promptly met the little dog that "never left his yard."

Since I was several hundred feet from his yard, and he was getting ready for the final move in his little campaign, I remembered Dad's directions. I waited until just the right moment and swung my helmet by the facemask. I caught the little pest right under the chin on a full swing. He made one more yap while he was airborne, and when he landed, he didn't move. I never broke stride and continued to walk home. I felt no remorse then, and I still don't. I love dogs and have never harmed one before or since, but this one caught me at the wrong time on the wrong day—supported with a full set of adult-sanctioned righteousness.

When I got home, I told my father what happened.

He listened, asked me again about my exact location, and said, "Okay."

Ten minutes later, the phone rang—and it was the nasty lady who owned the nasty dog.

He listened to her tale of me nearly murdering the dog. I was surprised the dog was alive; I was sure I'd killed him. After he could finally get a word in edgewise, Dad asked if I had come on her property to commit this crime. She said no; she'd found her dog in the road, right where I said it happened. I will always remember Dad's next remark.

He said, "Well, I guess you'll have to find another explanation since I have been assured by you that your dog has never attacked my son and never leaves your property. Perhaps you could call the dogcatcher for assistance. I'd be glad to call him for you, so long as we are both certain that the dog never leaves his property. Have a nice day." After he hung up and looked at my big happy smile, he reminded me that adults deserve respect until they've done something to demonstrate that they aren't fully worthy of it.

The dog never attacked me again, and I eventually did have that growth spurt that Mom predicted. Maybe it began that Saturday when I found out that simple justice can sometimes be enough.

FAMILY

Yesterday I walked alone among a distant group of my relatives I had never met before. I cannot describe the feeling of joy to discover that these too are connected to me in some deep seated way. This branch of my family is a very, very old one, perhaps some of the oldest living things on earth. They are intensely silent, massive, and brooding; it as though they were working on much greater mysteries than I could possible present to them.

I cannot prove in any sort of genealogical way that I come from the same family as the California redwoods, yet I am certain that I do. I have felt a similar certainty about other nonhuman living things once I got up next to them, and I cannot explain the power or logic. I am indifferent about the logic of the situation, but I am deeply moved by the power.

When I was a boy of ten or eleven, we took a day trip to the Audubon Society Preserve from Camp Mohawk. On the way, Pete Wallach stopped the truck we were all packed into on a narrow, hilly road. "Boys, climb out of the truck and look at these trees on either side of the road. They are one of the only stands of virgin timber left in Connecticut, and I think you'll be surprised at their size."

Wherever you are, Pete, thank you for that moment. The Cathedral Pines in Cornwall have been my spiritual anchoring place for most of my life since that day, ending with the moment when a tornado ran smack into them, undoing more than two hundred years of careful protection in fifteen minutes. I still mourn their passing.

The impact of really massive trees on me and on most people is a profoundly beautiful thing to watch or be part of. Children do not shout among the redwoods, and they didn't in Cornwall either. The exquisite hush their canopies hold provides a wonderfully safe, secure, and warm feeling that is not found anywhere else. Some of my more religious friends have described that feeling in the great churches of the world, but I have never felt it there, at least not to the same degree.

I am sure the people who passed me on the well-worn trails of Muir Woods thought I was in some sort of deeply emotional turmoil as they glanced at my face. If they really knew me, they would know that the freely flowing tears were the result of a limitless joy that I feel whenever I am in the presence of that kind of glorious beauty. I cannot stop my tears, and I am not especially motivated to try. It simply feels good to be there and know that the trees and I are connected.

I am certain we are connected because of that reliable emotional reaction. I feel it often but seldom to the intensity I did the day I walked among those giants. I was not surprised that it was there. They feel it too I think, but for them, it is the status quo.

There must be a wonderful serenity to realize that you were here before Columbus was born, any states here were united, the Mayans had begun their temples, or John Muir walked among them and felt what I felt that day.

I will try to return to these relatives of mine as often as I can, and I plan to visit their cousins the Sequoias since I suspect that I am from their stock too. I will return because I will always remember the swift finality at the end of the Cathedral Pines. I still lament that I did not go there more often. I know that we can undo the two thousand years of longevity of the redwoods and the sequoias as easily as I can walk among them, and I realize that the more violent force of nature can do it even easier. I will do what I can to prevent the untimely end of those trees, but standing among them is the best reminder of our actual significance in all the natural world, which is to say nearly none.

I was there for a few hours, and I am changed just as we are whenever we spend time appreciating where our roots began. I can go again and will, but I savor the time I went there first. And if it is the only time, I think it will sustain me.

THE LATEST LESSON
2008

Recently, a person I don't know very well, but who'd had the opportunity to watch me work, described me as a lifelong learner. I was delighted. I view myself the same way. I often am forced within the scope of my work to remember that everybody isn't wired with the expectation that each day brings us something that better prepares us for the next. I am always a little amazed whenever I am reminded of it.

I have known for a long time that I was programmed to be a perpetual learner by my mother. She was (and apparently still is) the ultimate teacher. She passed from this realm just three weeks ago, and I guess I am still adjusting. My friends who have lost both parents, regardless of age, tell me that the adjustment is perpetual. I am in no position to argue.

I have also known, perhaps for not as long, that my mother's lessons for me were often not overt or even consciously motivated. I believe that she understood what I needed in life and was programmed to try to help me get it. I think I was her learning lab, a place she could try out ideas about motivation and learn what worked and what didn't. Most of what she tried worked at least on me. I do not see much evidence that she worked the lessons as diligently for anyone else.

If I believe that almost all my relationship with my mother was designed, at least on her part, to keep me learning—and that many of the lesson plans took years to unfold—I wonder what the lesson was for me in her passing. I don't think this latest lesson was consciously created or executed. In fact, my mother's conscious awareness for more than the last year of her life was nearly nonexistent. I think the lesson was covert, buried under the sixty years she had me as a student. Surely she did not consciously think it up, but I believe it was there for me regardless. For three weeks now, I have been trying to figure out what it is.

I think maybe I get it. At least I get something connected to the plan that she set in motion fifty-five years ago and never let up on. Remarkably, this latest lesson could only be accomplished through her death. Somewhere in her deepest psyche, I believe she knew that.

To capture the essence of the lesson, I need to offer context in the broadest sense. For me, it started in grammar school. I was almost always the smallest kid in my class, certainly the smallest boy. When we filed into the auditorium for eighth-grade graduation, boys in one line, girls in the other, organized by height, I was first in my line. I realize now how hard my mother worked to bolster my self-esteem during this difficult portion of my childhood. She was always in my corner, always telling me that I could accomplish anything I wanted in life, but only if I was willing to work for it. No free passes. The difference between the current focus on self-esteem in raising children and the system my mother and father used is enormous. In the value set from both of my parents, the central theme was that achievement entitled you to feel good about yourself. You needed to earn the right; it was not granted simply because you existed.

When Mom was in her eighties, she liked to watch UConn women's basketball, mostly because they worked so hard. But she never could accept the practice of getting congratulatory handshakes from your teammates when you missed the first of two foul shots. She would never condone chastising or booing them, but unless you were successful, the best your teammates should do is just look away when you missed. It always bothered her.

So my mother became a one-woman taskforce to help me learn to achieve and thereby feel good about myself. As an educator, she knew not to push me into activities that didn't interest me, and fortunately for us both, lots of things interested me. During my freshman year of high school, I began to grow. In fact, I grew more than seven inches in fourteen months. It took another three years to regain most of my coordination. But the lingering questions about self-worth had already been established as my preadolescent value set was formed. Apparently, I still have them. I am not ashamed to admit that they are still there, but I am a bit surprised. I am always a little surprised when somebody tells me they like me—or when I can legitimately help someone—and they say so. I think my mother knew those doubts were still there, and it bothered her at least enough to motivate her to continue my lessons.

So here's what I think the latest lesson is. The people who surrounded me, held me up, and kept me going when my mother died have been the purveyors of the lesson, and my mother knew that they would be. They should not feel manipulated. They should feel honored.

The outpouring of care, concern, grief, and love that I received when my mother passed astounded me. It made me humble and powerfully grateful. When I expressed surprise at the response I got from my work associates, someone said, "What is it about 'We love you' that isn't clear to you?" In that simple, moving, deeply anchored question, I got the lesson. People think I am worthy, and it's okay for me to think I am too. I am not better than anyone else, simply worthy. For me, it'll always be about demonstrating worthy behavior, but it has always been that way for me.

Every card, every kind word, every note, every smile, and every tear meant more to me than I can ever express. It all helped me heal, and it all helped me learn.

You go, Ma!

SOAKED TO THE ASS AGAIN

SOAKED TO THE ASS AGAIN

First of all, for those readers whose delicate sensibilities are upset by the title of this piece, here is a bit of explanation. This and many of the other pieces in this collection are stories about Roger, Jack, and me on various and sundry fishing trips we have enjoyed together. We have been fishing together for more than thirty-five years, and it appears that only physical limitations will prevent us from doing it for the rest of our lives. As individuals, we are all relatively independent and often enjoy fishing alone as much as we do socially. We do not need each other to have a good time, yet we often prefer traveling together to great fishing places. More recently, we prefer finding ways to fish together from Roger's boat, which is large enough to accommodate us all—if we pay attention to each other's movement and watch our back casts.

Since the first time we fished together, we have resisted any pretense among us when we are together. We have each shown all of who we are to each other—good or bad, strong or weak—and apparently the good is enough to keep us compatible. Some of the manifestations of our lack of pretense are a certain joyful crudeness, especially in the area of graphic language. Our conversational subject matter would shock the sensibilities of most people, I think, especially women. Naturally, there are many exceptions to the above. Some people find our banter funny, even entertaining. Those who are especially astute or really listen would hear a very solid ethical and moral baseline to our crude language. I neither apologize nor advocate for our way of thinking and talking to each other. It is just how we do it, and that's been enough for us for all these years.

So the title of this piece is "Soaked to the Ass Again" because that is the phrase we have been using together for years. It captures for us the essence of our trips because no matter how much we plan to prevent it, sooner or later, we find ourselves in the position of getting drenched and being unable to do anything about it. I've tried to rename this certainty, but no euphemism gets the job done to my satisfaction. Since the core of our friendship has been straightforward and sometimes brutally honest, the title stands.

I think the three of us would agree that the best illustration of the STTAA phenomenon occurred on Lower Richardson Lake in the Rangeley region of Maine. We were in pursuit of landlocked salmon and native squaretail trout. The lake is very large, actually consisting of what used to be two separate lakes until Middle Dam was built in the thirties, raising the water level and connecting the two with a strip of water called the Narrows. One of the more interesting characteristics of the lake is that it is not uncommon for two separate and opposing weather patterns to exist on each of the halves of the lake simultaneously. So if you are in a small open boat placidly motoring along on the lower lake in very calm conditions, once you move up through the Narrows, you might find yourself in the middle of a twenty-mile-per-hour headwind, rollers to three feet, and soaking spray for all passengers each time the bow whacks into one of those rollers.

Why don't we turn around and go back to the lower lake? It's not quite that simple. When the boat you're riding in is only twelve feet long and the motor is only twenty horsepower, there will be a point in that "turnaround" move when the boat will be broadside to the waves. There is a reasonable certainty that waves that size will either roll the boat over or break over the side and fill the boat with breathtakingly cold water.

So in what seems now like a remarkably short period of time, the three of us were in a very tricky situation. The nearest real road was more than twenty miles away, the nearest people were twelve miles down the lake, and there were no other boats on the lake. It is that very remoteness that attracts us to places like Richardson, and we are always cognizant of the liabilities that accompany that attractiveness.

Jack was in the stern handling the motor, and Roger and I quickly moved to side-by-side positions in the center of the boat, leaning forward. Since all three of us know how to handle a boat pretty well, there wasn't too much need for verbal communication for any of us to know what to do. Jack knew that a certain amount of forward speed was necessary to maintain steerage and that a gradual turn, trying to nose the bow into the waves, was the way to keep us out of the water. So after a few short panicky moments, we settled into what we knew was the best plan for the conditions. The wind was blowing down a ten-mile-wide bay and really moving the water by the time it reached us at the downwind end.

Each time the bow of the boat smacked into one of those breaking rollers, a wall of spray would be thrown forward and to the side of the boat. The spray would suspend in the air for a second, and then the wind would catch it and blow it, full force, into Roger and me. It seemed totally incongruous that we could be out in a boat on such a beautifully clear day on such sparklingly clear water, totally soaked as if we had been fully immersed in the lake. To make it even more annoying and uncomfortable, Jack was relatively dry. Roger and I were acting more or less as a wind and water shield for him. Even though we knew better, it appeared to us that Jack was selecting the largest, most certain waves to get us wetter than necessary. And since we were already soaked to the skin, the impact of those waves served to lower our concern for Jack's welfare with each bone-chilling bath. Any of the three of us was fully capable of taking advantage of that situation to maximize the discomfort of the others, especially if there is some nautical or woodsmanship rule for us to hide behind. Roger and I were feeling more and more certain that Jack was endeavoring to do that because we each knew that we would have if given the chance.

It also seemed to us that he wasn't turning the boat as quickly as he could, prolonging our agony, which either of us would also try to do if we were in his seat. It is a lovely ballet of apparent concern for each other, finding a way to make the other guy really miserable without actually endangering him beyond discomfort and downright vindictive meanness. So, again without spoken words, Roger and I began to hatch a plan. We exchanged the knowing look of agreement and began to look for the right opportunity.

Jack had moved as far forward on his seat as he could, both for better boat balance and to hide more effectively behind his human windshield. It was apparent to Roger and me that he did not see our plan developing. Roger made the first move beautifully. He turned his head, taking the next spray bath directly down his neck, and screamed, "Turn the G__ D_____ boat around, you jerk—or risk having your scraggly butt thrown overboard."

As the rules of the situation required, Jack replied, "I was just trying to keep you both safe from capsizing, but if you think we can swing it around here, I'm ready to go for it."

As the boat swung around and into the next wave more fully, maximizing the spray wall, Roger glanced at me. I nodded. Once the spray went up, caught the wind fully and began to move toward our battered bodies, we both leaned way out to our respective sides of the boat, and the wall of water hit Jack fully in the face and chest. The timing was flawless—from years of preparation and practice—and driven by cold, wet anger and an overwhelming need for revenge.

The impact was a joy to behold. The force of the slap drove Jack all the way to back of his seat, lifting the bow higher as the boat continued its swing away from the wind. The cold and the surprise knocked the wind out of him with such swift finality that he turned white as a sheet and was unable to breathe for a few seconds. Despite his situation, he was forced to hang on to the tiller and turn the boat.

As we swung neatly into the safer downwind direction, our boat speed accelerated quickly. We shot safely back into calmer waters in less than two minutes. Once we got back into quieter water, I suggested beaching the boat to empty the water out of it and regain our composure.

Jack was not yet able to speak, but he turned toward shore. As we jumped out onto land and pulled the boat safely ashore, Roger and I couldn't hold back any more and laughed until we cried.

Jack steadily whispered, "You bastards, you bastards," which only added to our hysteria.

These are the moments we live the rest of the year for. This is why we go through the often-annoying difficulty to get to these places. These are the moments that hold us together as a team.

Each time we venture out to find these moments, we know with total certainty that the book of our travels will develop a new chapter captured, at least for us, within the phrase "soaked to the ass again."

THE BOYS

We first met in 1973 or 1974. I was working part-time at the Y, teaching adult "learn-to-swim" classes on Wednesday nights from seven until eight. Roger and Jack came into the pool at eight to teach the certifying scuba course. I occasionally hung around, largely because scuba often attracted young women who used the course to meet men or prepare for vacations. The general clientele of the scuba class was socially, financially, and sometimes physically more elevated than my adult swim class. Over time, I began to help with the survival swimming skills portion of the scuba curriculum because neither of the instructors could actually swim worth a damn. They often joked that their early skill development in scuba was caused by the inordinate amount of time they spent underwater while merely trying to swim. Rather than resist, they decided to specialize in the environment under the surface.

Anyhow, that's where we met. As is often the case when a fisherman talks with new acquaintances, fishing came up early and became a regular part of our conversation. All three of us are within a year or two of age, and it became apparent that much of our youth and young adulthood had been focused on the outdoors generally and fishing specifically. Without ever having met previously, we had fished much of the same waters in northwest Connecticut and in a few other places as well. At the time, I was more or less strictly a fly fisherman. My two new friends expressed interest in learning more about it, but their initial attempts were not very successful. I don't know who made the first suggestion to go fishing, but it doesn't matter. Plans were set, and we've been going ever since.

Another tradition was spawned from those sessions on Wednesday nights. It was already a tradition for Roger and Jack, and I simply adopted it. The primary reason they taught the course on Wednesday nights was to get out of their respective houses and make enough money at it to buy beer and sandwiches after class. They described it as having a weekend night in the middle of the workweek. My guess is that since 1974 we have averaged forty-five or forty-seven Wednesday nights together per year. For more than forty years, going out with the boys on Wednesdays has been an anchor in my life.

How we spend our time on Wednesdays has evolved as we have aged and our fortunes have changed. Now we have it down to a comfortable science. For a long time (until knees and motivation waned) somewhere around October 1, we joined a few other pals and played wallyball at the local health club. After the games, we went out for pizza and beer. We took a break from wallyball in early December and met in my barn to throw darts. Then we went out for pizza and beer. Wallyball resumed in early January and ran for ten or twelve weeks. After each of those game nights, we would go out for pizza and beer. In late March and early April, we might fit in a couple of darts weeks until daylight savings time (followed by the usual), when we switched to fishing until dark on Wednesday nights. After dark, we'd go for pizza and beer. That lasted until October when it started over again.

The number of guys who have joined in on these festivities has varied in number and person. Now there are the three of us and often a couple of others—at least for the pizza and beer. We play cribbage as we eat our pizza and drink our beer. We have never tired of this routine, and I don't expect that we ever will. My first wife never approved of our Wednesday-night activities, and she never gave up trying to get me quit. I bet it still annoys her. My lady now understood the deal before she married me. She truly loves my friends and fully understands the power and significance of Wednesday nights. The realization on my part of her approval and acceptance of the event contributed to my decision to ask her to marry me.

In terms of backgrounds away from fishing and our love of the outdoors, we really don't have much in common—or at least we didn't at the start. Both of my pals went to trade school after high school while I spent the next eight years in college, off and on. Our family backgrounds don't match very well, and our childhoods were somewhat different. Since we knew we had very different outlooks, I guess we knew from the start that we would have to try to accept one another's differences if we wanted to go fishing together. Fishing was our early catalyst. Oh, we constantly hammer each other over our differences, and that process has clearly become our way of demonstrating acceptance and affection.

None of us is sure when we went on our first fishing trip together, but it was a long time ago. We started with trips to Vermont to Jack's ski club's lodge in the off-ski season. The trips got longer and farther, extending to Maine, Cape Cod, and Martha's Vineyard. Like our routines on Wednesday nights, the trips have developed a regimen that we adhere to pretty consistently.

We prefer having a place to stay that is remote from other people. In Maine, that places us on an island, reachable only by boat, in a small cabin with enough room to cook, sleep, throw darts, and sit on a marginally screened porch and listen to the loons. At the Cape, it places us in a housekeeping cottage with similar features to the one in Maine, at the end of the line of cottages.

We have the process of preparing for, moving into, and living in these places down to a neat science. The Maine deal is much more difficult and complex because there are no available services nearby; supplies and planning tend to be more elaborate. The Cape is easier since we trailer a boat to each of our favorite launching areas each day; picking up supplies is easy. We do Maine in the spring and the Cape in the fall. In each of those locations, we have found the beauty and fish that make us happy.

In both places, it is clear that we might find different and even better fishing with different tactics. While we say we are going to try new ideas every year, somehow we just revert to the old spots—fished the way we have fished them before—with approximately the same gratifying success. A commonality among the three of us is that when we find a way that makes us happy, we stay with it—even though we might elevate it if we tried. Nope, no sense in risking how good it is now.

We have changed our system when it did not serve us adequately. We used to go to the Rangeley Lakes region of Maine. The fishing was never that overwhelming, but the isolation and sheer natural beauty was awesome. Eventually, the isolation became less certain. It was clear that our days at Lower Dam were numbered the first time a pickup truck dropped off a load of fishermen at our favorite area. It takes more than ten hours to reach our Maine destination now, and the last fifteen miles are on dirt roads. We are twenty-five miles from anything like a town and nearly fifty miles from a hospital or other large services—our idea of paradise.

And so our time together continues. We are all getting a bit long in the tooth, and sometimes we have speculative discussions about which of us will be the first to go. That discussion is usually followed by a plea to make certain that the survivors get the deceased guy's fishing stuff. Over the years, each of us has amassed a collection of fishing equipment that is impressive individually and would be overwhelming collectively.

Wednesday nights are still sacrosanct—at least when we are all in town at the same time. The pizza and beer are still good, shadowed only by the sense of comfort and belonging that the company provides. For most of my adult life, it has been a consistent, reliable source of quiet joy.

DIAMONDS IN THE ROUGH

I've tried to write this particular story several times over the years and have never been satisfied. At first, I thought that perhaps the event couldn't be captured in words. Then I thought that it could, but I lacked the skills to do it. Since I'm back at it again, I guess I don't really believe that either.

I suppose the significance of the event for me is as much due to the place as to the event. It happened at Upper Dam in Maine. The actual dam separates Mooselookmeguntic Lake from Upper Richardson Lake. There has been a dam there for a long time. It was once an integral part of the logging business, later a source of waterpower, and now part of an elaborate series of dams, lakes, and rivers that are controlled by the Union Waterpower Company for many applications.

The pool below the dam is called, not surprisingly, Upper Dam Pool, and it has been famous since Teddy Roosevelt vacationed there to fish for brook trout. For many years, it was a mecca for rich "sports" who would stay in the many cabins there, fishing the sluiceways below the dam or hiring guides to row them out into the huge pool with its swirling and intricate currents. Several classic fly patterns were invented there, most by a woman named Carrie Stevens, the wife of a guide. There is a plaque commemorating her accomplishments on the path outside what was her camp.

We were there because the place is simply breathtakingly beautiful. It long ago lost its luster and fame as the best "brookie fishing" in America. It is largely overgrown now, and it requires a really active imagination to picture the hotels that were once at the dam and on Richardson near Mosquito Brook. The foundations are still there and are fun to explore. We go for the same reasons the first ones did: pristine lakes and forests and the potential for good fishing. The quarry is landlocked salmon now as much as trout (maybe more).

We used to stay in a small cabin on Metallak Island on Upper Richardson with a history all its own. It was the main salon of a steam ferry that ran from South Arm to Upper Dam during the area's heyday. The location was perfect for Roger, Jack, and me. It was very comfortable and very secluded, reachable only by boat. It was common practice for us to hop in the boat and run up to Upper Dam to fish the evening hatch or whenever else we could. With the ice-cold sluices pouring into the pool, the fish could be there at any time. It was always an exciting place to fish because the chances of tying into a heavy fish were always good. Additionally, the place was simply gorgeous. I will never tire of sitting up on the bank next to the dam and watching the fishermen, fish, birds, the occasional bear, and the giant sky.

We spent a morning on the platforms at the ends of the sluiceways, casting into the wild waters. I can't remember if I was successful or not. Probably not especially or I would remember it better. When my arm got tired, I climbed back up the ladders and rails to the bank above the pool and sat in my waders on the grass to relax and watch. There is a certain peace that flows over me in that place that doesn't happen in too many other places I know about.

I was lost in the reverie of watching the artistic ballet of the casters below me when the shadow of a very large bird passed over my head. A large eagle was gliding over the pool, obviously hunting. Jack, who was fishing below me, seemed not to notice it, being engrossed in his casting. While the pool is a pretty place to fish, the water is very dangerous. It's usually a good idea to keep your mind on what you are doing when you're out on the casting platforms.

I watched as this incredible hunter nearly hovered over the fast-moving water. In the blink of an eye, he folded his wings back and speared toward the water. With a small splash, he emerged with a very large salmon. It looked like something he did easily, many times a day. In reality, he may only be successful every few days or so, but it looked easy. As he began to rise from the water, I watched a wicked struggle develop. The fish was too large to be lifted easily, and the eagle had not gotten a good grip with the one talon he used. The fish flapping, the water from the dive soaking the feathers of the bird, and the weight of the fish all contributed to the fact that the eagle simply could not get sufficient altitude to get out of danger. The morning sun illuminated this drama for me with remarkable clarity. Every color was vivid, every movement evident.

With incredible strength and resolve, the bird rose slowly above the pool. He struggled up thirty or forty feet, and it was apparent that he might lose his dinner at any instant. In my mind, what followed was in slow motion, although I am sure it was but a flash of movement in the moment. The eagle dropped the fish on purpose, snapped into a somersault to dry off, and dove, picking up the falling fish about a foot from the water. With a better grip—and without the water he had shed—he flew directly and purposefully to a tall treetop at the foot of the pool and rested.

It was a remarkable display of aerial manipulation, calculation, and timing. I was just lucky enough to be in the right place at the right time. While I watched the eagle eat his catch, Jack climbed up and sat with me.

"Rather pleasant morning," he said.

"Yup. Did you see the bird?"

"What bird?"

"You missed an amazing event. I'm not sure that I can describe it to you and do it justice. I'll try."

I replayed the scenario for him, taking my time, trying to select my words carefully because I wanted accuracy, not exaggeration. I am more than capable of exaggeration, especially if it'll enhance a story, but this one was different. Exaggerating here would be equivalent to inflating the report of a great historic event. I showed him where the eagle was eating the salmon. I guess I told the story a little differently than usual because he didn't say anything for a long time after I stopped.

He told me I was a very lucky man, to be there at all, to have a day like that, and to see the eagle catch and recatch a salmon. "I'll bet you'll never forget it."

"I bet you're right. Because the part that is burned into my mind was the shower of diamond water droplets that flew off the bird when he let the fish go. The sun caught them perfectly, and they made an exploding rainbow of color. The eagle may have caught the fish, but I'm the one who got the prize."

And people sometimes ask me how I can go fishing and feel satisfied about sometimes not catching any. Really?

CANAL FISH

Among the three of us, I am clearly the novice when it comes to saltwater fishing. Roger and Jack grew up on Long Island Sound and on the Cape, spending lots of childhood vacation time there and then going to the salt water on their own as soon as they could drive themselves there. I too had my share of adventure as a kid in Long Island Sound.

As a young adult, I married into a family of would-be fishermen. I have spent plenty of time chasing the birds that chase the bait chased by the bluefish. But compared to Roger and Jack, my experience in the salt was relatively limited. They know how and when to fish with bait and what kind to use. They know about other quarry besides blues, especially striped bass. They approach the sport with a great more variety than I do, and I am happy to go with them and learn what they know.

One of the real attractions is that they don't like boredom much. We might troll for a while, but if we don't get a fish or two, it doesn't take long for one of us to get agreement to a different tactic. Each of us has uttered, "As long as I'm not catching anything, I might as well enjoy the process." We justify switching to fishing differently even when the new tactic is clearly not the most likely successful idea.

Related to their desire for variety is their desire to fish interesting places. It so happens that my early saltwater experiences were limited to Long Island Sound off Bridgeport or neighboring Fairfield, and the water there isn't very interesting in terms of variety. Once I began going with Roger and Jack, who fish more around the Norwalk Islands, whole new vistas opened up for me. Tides became more significant, and "fishing the rips" was much more exciting than trolling. Overall, there was more to know, more water and conditions to read, and more variables to take into consideration. In short, it was more fun.

So when the boys suggested a trip to Cape Cod, I was eager to go. The Cape is an area with a tremendous variety of conditions, quarry, and potential. It has a mystique all its own, and both my pals are well versed in its allure. Since then, we have had several extended trips, including trips to Martha's Vineyard to fish for October bluefish.

I think one other attractive aspect of our time fishing the Cape is related to boating knowledge. We fish out of a solid seventeen-foot boat with enough horsepower to get up and go when you need it. In our freshwater excursions, the conditions are much more predictable and generally much calmer. In the salt, you'd better know what you are doing—or you can be in a world of worry in a remarkably short time. Tide and current changes, when combined with a strong breeze, can create moderately dangerous conditions in a matter of moments, and the fishermen need to be paying attention to environmental cues constantly. The fun comes from the fact that those same cues are the ones that tell you where and when the fish will be; there are benefits to paying attention to what's going on around you.

The last variable in this formula are the fish themselves. Bluefish and stripers are some of the more effective predators in the sea, and they seldom miss an opportunity to capitalize on conditions that are favorable to them. When it all works out right—and the fisherman are in the right place at the right time— the result is some of the most exhilarating action I have ever experienced. While the windows of opportunity are relatively short and rare, the payoff is exceptional; it can keep guys like us going back over and over again.

Several years ago, our schedules were such that it made sense for us to spend the full week we normally devote to freshwater trips to Maine on the Cape instead. It was October, and most of the overcrowding that sometimes plagues the Cape was over. We rented a housekeeping cabin for off-season rates and had most of the areas we fished to ourselves or nearly so. We arrived in late afternoon, and after moving into the cabin, we had time to go "fish the canal" after dark.

The canal is the Cape Cod Canal, which actually makes the Cape an island. It is cut through the most western part of the Cape, near the mainland and is a remarkable construction achievement. It is deep and wide, and huge boats travel it in both directions, thereby avoiding having to sail all the way around Cape Cod to get to and from Boston Harbor to points south and west. Since boats are restricted from fishing in the Canal, it is fished from shore. A wide, street-lit road raised above the canal on both sides is closed to auto traffic for most of the year. When the tide is right and the stripers are in, it is an exciting place to fish. Since stripers tend to be more active at night, it is a very popular place to fish after dark.

Our plan was to drive to a parking area near the highway bridge and walk up the canal, watching for schools of surface-feeding bass. The tide had just changed, and a strong current was beginning to build out in the canal. When we began our walk, we heard the unmistakable sound of a tail slap somewhere out in the middle. The potential for a memorable evening was good, and I was especially excited because I had never fished the canal before. I had been regaled with canal stories for years. If half of what I'd been told was true, I might experience some very exciting fishing.

We each took a spot on the rocks that comprise the banks of the canal. We were perhaps a hundred yards apart and fishing in the dark, although the streetlights did allow us to see each other dimly. I was carrying a large surf-casting rod and a smaller lightweight saltwater spinning rod. Frankly, the experience was a little frightening—and very exciting. Standing alongside this water as it flew by in full tidal flow, I saw huge wash-bucket-sized swirls as big bass nailed hapless baitfish trapped by the fast-rising tide. It was exciting and more than a little unnerving. I decided to fish with the smaller rod because I was more familiar with it, and I thought I would be able to see most of my casts with it. I knew I would not have to cast too far to be over good fish, and I chose control over strength. I still have doubts about whether I made the right decision.

The current flowed from the right to the left that night (it changes direction each time the tide changes). After the first cast or two with the Rapala, it became evident that the fish eve weren't going to be that easy to catch. The water conditions were unlike any I was used to casting over because the current was flying by so strongly. By the time I reeled up the slack from each cast, the lure would already be several yards down the current. Placing the lure exactly where you wanted it was impossible—and unnecessary. It was blind fishing, and my heart was pounding long before I missed the first strike. After that one, I was far more alert. I had the next fish on for a moment or two before I lost it. In that brief time, I realized that I was in a whole new world of fishing. The combination of a fifteen-pound fish out in that incredible current on a relatively light rod with only a fifteen-pound test line was an awesome experience. I knew that I should probably stop and switch to the larger rod, but the action was too exciting to take the chance of missing it. I stayed with the lighter rod.

I actually saw the strike when the bass hit the Rapala, but I wasn't exactly sure where the lure was until I set the hook. Since I'd already missed two strikes, I set that one several times. Even with all the adrenaline, I was not ready for what happened. The big bass boiled on the surface once and then simply took off downstream. I tried to slow him with the rod fully stressed and the drag at the breaking point, but it had no effect on the fish whatsoever. I stood there transfixed, listening to the line scream off the reel against the drag for quite some time until it finally dawned on me that the fish would soon run all the line off my reel and break the line.

I scrambled over the large wet rocks and the seaweed. I fell repeatedly, and when I got back on my feet, the line was slack. I was sure the fish was gone—probably with my Rapala. As I cursed and began to reel in my line rapidly, the line came up tight again against the fish. The dance began all over again.

The actual elapsed time from hookup to completion was fifteen or twenty minutes, but it felt like hours. When the fish began to tire, I was already exhausted. I reeled in about half the line, and the fish saw the shore lights clearly. It was gone again, and all I could do was hold on. After repeating that scenario a couple more times, I moved the fish into shallow water directly in front of me and saw him clearly for the first time. The picture is vivid—and I hope it never dims. In the combination of the streetlights and my ragged breathing, he looked huge. He was also only hooked by one treble hook and not very securely. In one desperate move, against all the sporting rules of fishing, I horsed him behind a large rock mostly out of the water and pounced on him. I sat in the puddle of water with my fish and waited for both of us to revive a little.

When I could move again, I measured the fish on my rod. I was disappointed to find that it was only thirty inches. Nothing alive and thirty inches long could do to a two-hundred-pound man what this creature had just done. Without fully lifting the fish from the water, I slid the remaining hook free and released him back to current. He hung there for a moment, gathering strength—and then he was gone in the same sort of swirl we had started with.

I sat there for a long time: partially wanting to regain my composure, partially hoping I might not. The current and the feeding fish continued all around me in the eerie darkness, and I really felt like a part of the scene. There was no feeling of triumph over nature—only a deeply reverent respect for a system that I knew very little about. It all made sense to the creatures for whom this was a constant life-or-death struggle, and I knew I was privileged to have been even a momentary part of it.

After I got some of my wind back, I climbed up the bank and walked back up the road, watching for the rest of my equipment. That's when I realized how far I'd chased the fish. It was a long, long way. When I got back to my stuff, Roger and Jack were waiting. Neither said too much, and I was glad. One risks sounding a little demented if one lets the situation get to him while he tries to explain it. I didn't want to risk that, especially with the rest of the week of living with these guys.

Jack said, "I saw you take off and figured you must have had your hands full."

"Yup," I answered.

"Then, when you went out of sight, I figured it must have been a pretty good fish. When I got here to your big rod and realized what you were fishing with, I figured that you were probably in for more than you bargained for."

"Yup," I answered.

"You land him?"

"Yup."

He shined his flashlight in my face for a moment and looked in my eyes.

"Oh," he said. "So, how'd you like fishing the canal?"

"It was pretty good," I answered.

We walked mostly in silence back to the car, still hearing the fish slapping out in the current. They had each caught and released a couple of fish around twenty inches, and I got no argument about the size of mine. It was obvious that there were plenty of larger fish in the canal that night.

As we were pulling back in to our cabin Roger said, "There's no point in trying to tell somebody about your first good fish in the canal at night. It's something you have to experience. Maybe you'll write about it someday, but you'll never capture it completely."

He was right. I haven't, but I am glad I tried.

MEDITATION IN CATHEDRALS OF OUR OWN * AUGUST 1990

I rode down to the Housatonic River to fish last night. It's no big deal for me to do that; I've been doing it for thirty years. I haven't done it in quite some time though, and I took my time because the ride is a part of the fishing for me. It's part of the serenity and peace.

There are several different routes I can take, but all of them run in a northwesterly direction, going around or over Mohawk Mountain. Last night I chose to travel the College Street route. I have no idea why it is called College Street since there isn't one on it—and it doesn't lead to one either. My guess is that a college bought land in the area, maybe for natural history or agricultural research, although I have absolutely no evidence to support this hunch. Somehow that doesn't bother me, and while I am mildly curious about it, I don't intend to get the mystery cleared up anytime soon.

On a semisunny, muggy evening in June, College Street is beautiful. To reach the junction of Great Hill Road, I went past the big, beautiful marsh, the sheep farm, the old beaver dam that has driven the Cornwall road crews crazy for years, the occasional house, and the intersection with Flat Rocks Road (which is a different route I take when I'm in a hurry). It is reassuring that even though I haven't traveled this route since last fall, nothing has changed much. Houses have been worked on a bit, and maybe a building lot had the trees cut back a little, but generally it's the same place it's been since I was a boy at summer camp. For me, that sameness is a cause for quiet rejoicing.

Great Hill Road is impressive. At least it is from the College Street intersection northward. It is one of the longest, steepest hills one can travel down anywhere in northwest Connecticut, and that alone is pretty neat, but the kicker is that it slides so gracefully into Mohawk Valley. At the bottom, for perhaps only four hundred yards, the road slices the valley floor. The view to the south is so peaceful that I can feel the tension from my lousy city job melting out of my mind and body. A low ridge forms the western side of the valley. The road runs along the eastern side of the ridge, and if you don't turn off, it will eventually take you past the ski area at Mohawk Mountain and out to Route 4.

I turn off Great Hill and slide over the ridge to the next valley, which I call the Valley of the Cathedral Pines, although I doubt if it is actually called that. The road takes me right through what used to be called Cathedral Pines. It was once a very special place, unlike any I know anywhere else. I would rank it up there with the majesty of Yosemite and the miracle of the redwoods. Here, tucked into the side of this little ridge, right next to the village of Cornwall, stood a grove of pines nearly two hundred years old. They were protected from lumbering, disease, and development by the people of this village for all those years, and they were absolutely awesome. They stood straight and incredibly tall. Dark, peaceful, and silent, their presence was so strong that children whispered when they walked among those trees without anyone having to tell them to do so. They have been at the center of my soul since the first time I saw them. They were my church, my sanctuary, and my solace from the rest of the harsh realities of life.

And then, through the incredible force of nature, a tornado destroyed them in fifteen minutes. I guess it is some comfort that natural forces took the Cathedral pines, rather than man, but it isn't much comfort.

I rode through the ruins of the pines on my way to the river five days after their destruction. I cannot express the pain and loss I felt. I have experienced loss before—of loved ones, possessions, and relationships—and those hurts eventually turn numb, but this loss still hurts. It hurt that night I drove through them just after they were gone, and it hurt again last night. The night right after the storm, I tried to walk the old paths, but they were blocked by the slaughtered trees. I got back into the car and drove the remaining five miles down to river to meet Roger and Jack.

When I parked in the lot at the river, the boys were already there. I saw Roger first. Among the three of us, Roger is the least effusive. But like a man who loves music but won't dance, his awareness and insight into the human condition is often exceptional.

As I got out of my car that night, he looked at me and said, "Aw, man, you came down through the Cathedral pines, didn't you? What would make you do a thing like that to yourself?"

Roger had not seen the pines since their destruction, but the local media had reported their loss. He knew me well enough to take one look at me and see the pain and know where it came from. I tried to explain that I had to go and see for myself—even though I didn't really know why. I guess he understood enough to not pursue it with me then.

I still travel through the ruins of the pines. I guess I still hope to extract something from them. Besides, just after the pines is what I think is the prettiest valley anywhere. It also runs north and south like Mohawk Valley, but it is more diverse. The presence of Cornwall Village on its northern edge adds greatly to the pastoral beauty of the scene. I guess I appreciate the valley more now that the trees are gone from the hillside, and I am never disappointed with the view, regardless of weather or season.

The answer to Roger's question is becoming more evident to me as I grow older and am more and more attracted to the important places in my world. I guess I am willing to subject myself to the pain I still feel from the ruins on the hillside because the rest is enough to renew me. The pain is my problem—a product of my own making—as is the peace and contentment I feel from those two valleys, the mountain, and the river. It's a package deal, and I won't give up on it all to avoid the hurt from the loss of the trees. Maybe they taught me how to do that. Maybe I do that to myself because they taught me about surviving by taking it all together and growing stronger as a result. Getting the message about survival was more important than how I got it, and it isn't very compelling to spend much more time trying to figure it all out.

*"Meditations in Cathedrals of Our Own" is a portion of a song lyric from Billy Joel. The line is actually: "I believe there comes a time for meditation in cathedrals of our own." I thought of the Cathedral pines the first time I heard it—and every time since.

DEFINING
MOMENTS

THE SMELL OF AN ORANGE
1993

The memories are all cloudy now. It was so many years ago. Each person who told me the story in bits and pieces—a glimmer of clarity followed by the old safe cloudiness—told it a bit differently. The best was the day at the beach house when my daughter was fifteen or sixteen. Cory was reading Latin in her grandfather's sitting room, which was consistent with her insatiable quest for learning.

"What'cha readin', Cor?" Gido asked when he sat in his favorite seat. He was always interested in the schooling of his grandchildren, perhaps because he had been unable to get the kind of formal schooling himself that a powerful mind like his sought.

"Latin," she replied. After a little thought, she asked, "Did you ever have to take Latin when you went to school, Gido?"

His surprised laugh wasn't bitter or sad. "No," he told her. "I never went to school. I always was working." After a long silence, he spoke softly and quietly about his childhood—from his earliest memories of anything solid. Cory and I instantly knew we were hearing something he had never told before. We knew we were hearing the story of the miraculous exodus from Syria through the eyes of an eight-year-old boy who had been building this narrative for nearly seventy years.

I looked frantically around the room for a tape recorder to capture his. Why we were honored this way is still unclear to me, but I would not trade that moment for anything. I have always been deeply fascinated by the strength of the oral tradition—and by the fact that, for centuries, all that was known by anyone was told to him or her by someone else. And so I calmed my panicky search for a way to record this narrative and thought that this story was to hear as it was in this place, at this time because the elder who chose to tell it felt it was the time.

Sorrowfully, I cannot remember all the details ten years later, but I realize the details aren't what the story is really about. Various family members had heard bits and pieces here and there, and together they had built a relatively reliable story line, but this time, it was told wholly from start to finish.

The basic facts went something like this: They left their village in Syria because their mother had died (from an infection from a rusty nail in her foot) and their father, who was already in America, had sent for them.

My father-in-law and his older brother traveled with a group of other friends and relatives. They were eight and ten years old. The older brother had already assumed many of the duties and all the responsibility of their missing father, and he took his little brother on the journey to America. To this day, they both feel strongly that those roles were clear.

The trip to the boat to take them to America is a blur of border crossings and stealth. It is apparent that they walked most of the way or rode in wagons. It is also apparent that they had little or no food and were on the verge of starvation throughout the entire journey. You don't gather the full impact of the walk until you look at a map and realize that they left from Syria and sailed from Marseille, France. The distance alone is astounding—until you realize the topography of the trip. That they made it at all is a miracle, yet the story is not uncommon among many of the immigrants who came to America in the 1920s.

That the trip is still a blur for Gido is not surprising from either a simple recall or a psychological point of view. It took a long time, although the full duration is unclear. By the time the boys finally got to America, they were two years older than when they left, but it is unclear how long they waited to get on the boat in France. It is also unclear who actually made the arrangements.

As I listened to this amazing memory, transfixed by its full significance, I was struck by something that brought this man's whole life into focus for me. He is known throughout Connecticut for his generosity and assistance to others. His house is always overfilled with food. There is always too much of everything. Not surprisingly, he has been a grocer and produce man his whole life. I cannot recall a time that there wasn't fruit, oranges especially, in his home. His wife is still considered a culinary wizard. When his friends and family gather, it is to eat. There might be other reasons for the gathering, but the absolutely certain behavior would be the preparation and enjoyment of food.

Now, hearing of the starvation of that journey from the view of a ten-year-old boy whose life's values were still forming, the die was cast. Food for this man didn't—and doesn't—mean the same thing as it does for the rest of us. For us, it is a means to satiate hunger or enjoy favorite flavors. For him, it a symbol of security and safety. And more than anything else, it is a symbol of America.

While the story was cloudy in terms of detail, the sensory images were crystal clear. Today he will not eat butter because of the rancid smell he has associated with it while searching for food in garbage cans. He can remember the feel of the clothing they wore, the cold they felt, and most clearly the smells of food they could not have.

I have known this remarkable man for more than thirty years, loved him as a second father for nearly twenty. I have seen him suffer through his own inability to understand the behavior of his grandchildren who do not react to prosperity as he thought they would or should. I have heard his pain when he would lament that these children do not understand and respond to the power of real family. I have often been perplexed by his lack of a big-picture perspective. His mind is a straight-line machine, and throughout his life, it has served more than it has harmed him. I do not think like him in very many ways, and it has taken several years for us to find a place in which to really understand each other.

Nearly all the uncertainty I ever had about who this guy really is was removed that day, there in his house, hearing this story. It has been a permanent part of my mind ever since, and I consider it one of life's real treasures, which was granted to me for reasons I am not sure of and simply don't need to question. I was there. It was told to Cory and me. Pure and simple.

By the time he was nearing the end of this narrative, talking about docking in Providence, Rhode Island, we were in the kind of awe that I am sure American Indian children felt listening to the stories of the beginning of the world from their elders. I was not prepared for the last image, and its impact on me was intensely powerful.

He said, "Once we got to America, there were several days before we could get off the boat. But sometimes we could come up on the deck and look at the wharf and see what America looked like. I can remember looking through the wire fencing below the railing of the boat.

"And I remember that one day we were all in a crowd around the railing, and I was in front. Somehow we had raised the money to buy a basket of fruit from the dock vendors below us on the wharf. I still couldn't get over the fact that there was a whole bunch of them and they all had food and were actually able to sell it and all the rich Americans would buy it. Somebody found a rope and threw the money down to the vendor who tied the basket of fruit to the rope and it was hoisted up carefully right past my face as I looked through the fence. As the basket was emptied by our group, somebody behind me reached over and around my shoulders with a large orange in their hands and peeled it right in my face and placed a section of it in my mouth. Nothing I have eaten in my life before or since tasted like that orange and the smell of that flavor will always stay in my head.

It was the smell of plenty, the smell of freedom, the smell of America. I will never forget it, never."

It seems entirely appropriate to me that the story of the smell of that orange, which he will never forget, is something I will never forget. That's how all the good stories in life should be. They cannot—and should not—be the same for the listener as they are for the teller. But the impact should be unforgettable because we need the lessons from the good stories to live our lives the right way.

It isn't every day that one story so completely clarifies a man's life for the listener. These are the days and the stories in life we must rejoice and preserve.

ELIXIR

I realize as I begin to write this that I don't know his actual name. In my time of knowing him, he was always called Tofie. I am sure that was a nickname because it was common among the Arabic community to replace actual names with alternates, sometimes to ease pronunciation, sometimes because of a distinguishing behavior, like most nicknames are earned. Anyway, I knew him as Tofie, and I don't know why he was called that.

I was an outsider married into the Syrian community, and in those early years, when I was still in my teens, I wasn't especially comfortable with the Arabs—and they weren't especially comfortable with me. Not only was I not Arabic, I wasn't even Italian, Spanish, Greek, or anything Mediterranean. I was Irish and more than a little arrogant. I was resistant to accepting their culture because I felt that to do so was disloyal to my own. As I said, I was still in my teens.

Tofie was painter. Not a painter of canvas, a painter of houses. I got to know him a bit because he was the painter that my father-in-law used for all his properties. My young wife and I were renting from Dad, so Tofie came to paint the apartment. I learned later that Tofie didn't always have a sterling reputation as a warm, supportive family man, but he was kind and friendly to me. He was one of several in my wife's family circle who attempted to treat me like an adult, purely on faith and goodwill since I had done nothing to earn that status. So even the simplest cordiality meant a lot to me, and I must have shown my appreciation somehow because Tofie always acknowledged my presence warmly in later years.

After my wife and I'd been married for a while, it was announced that there was to be a Saint George's Day dance. Up until then, Saint George wasn't especially high on the holy hit parade, but there were about ten guys in the church who were named George and who liked to party. They got together, pooled resources, and threw a party, only nominally related to the celebration of Saint George.

I wasn't thrilled about going to this dance, but I was interested in hearing the music. A group of young men from Danbury came down to play. I knew I would have the opportunity to listen to new rhythms and maybe get the hang of that weird twelve-tone scale, which was so different from my own. I convinced my wife to sit near the band, which was relatively easy because she had originally been betrothed to one of the guys in the band in her early childhood, and he was always a bit of a heartthrob for her.

Naturally, all the big shots of the Arabic community turned out for this event, and it was fun to see each family group gather and grow as more and more people arrived. By that time in his life, Tofie was mostly retired because his small body was shot. *Wizened* would best describe him that night. He was bent over from arthritis, and his hips were so deteriorated that he could only sort of shuffle instead of actually walk. He arrived late, and his family made the obligatory fuss over him that the patriarch of each family was supposed to receive. He was assisted into the room by one of his young grandsons, which added to the patriarchal image.

It made me really sad to see Tofie so fragile. Maybe it was because he had been kind to me or because my own father had been a painter, but I was projecting my own feelings about Dad into Tofie. I spent the next few minutes—from a safe distance— watching him slowly move into a chair, obviously in pain, but still trying to maintain the dignity that his position required. Finally he was ready, and we all waited for the priest to bless the food and gathering and offer the compulsory nod to good old Saint George. About one nanosecond after he was finished with his blessing, the drum began a solo rhythm pattern—perhaps two thousand years old—and I saw a miracle unfold before my eyes.

The sound of that drum went through Tofie like a shot. His head snapped up and forward, and a mystical current of energy straightened his spine. His shoulders squared, and his chest rose and projected forward. There were already dancers on the floor even before the other instruments joined in, and by the time they did, Tofie was a fully transfigured man. There was no way to describe him except large. The normal rules of physical size perceptions had been suspended, and he was functioning with an energy source this simple Irish kid did not understand but could not deny. I will never forget it. It retaught me what I'd always known intellectually—but had never experienced emotionally—that we have within us the capability to function from any number of different energy sources and that music was one of the passwords to enable the power to do so. The effect on me was not unlike the effect on Tofie, only less evident to others. Since that night in that church hall, I have been chasing the elixirs of life that we can all access. Each time I find one, I think of Tofie.

Tofie danced all night. He led dances, followed other leaders, laughed, and sang. There was absolutely no denying that the music of his homeland infused within him a joy and energy source that no medication we could invent could ever accomplish. The joy was the thing I remember most. I think it is tied up in a whole bunch of different power sources like ethnic identity, community roles and reputations, inherited instincts, and personal long-term memories. Had Tofie's doctors been there, I am sure they would have been in shock, because from the nonspiritual world of medicine, Tofie was clearly unable to dance all night. But he did. All night. I was there. My guess is that he would have been bedridden for days after the dance— and that he didn't care if he was. Once the music ended, it was back to the old reality and that was that. But the joy was still there, buried deep until the next dose of elixir freed it.

I have seen this phenomenon again several times since the Saint George's Day dance, and now it is safe to say that I am sort of searching for it. The other incidents of it have often been associated with ethnic music, although not every time. I went to college with a guy whose parents came to America from Scotland. He was always a bit ashamed of them because the lacked the savoir faire that he thought American parents should have. He said that he did not embrace the Scottish culture and customs and was a little derisive of his parents, especially his father, because they did. In fact, by the time I knew him, his relationship with his father was not good because his farther felt that Ken didn't have enough personal discipline and "backbone." All of us suffered from that malady in those days of Vietnam protests and government resistance, but Ken had added to that the fact that he said he rejected his heritage. It is no wonder that when his father died, he and Ken were barely on speaking terms.

I found out from Ken and other friends who went to the funeral that Ken was in pretty bad shape over the sudden loss of his father, contributed to as much from guilt as grief. The funeral was done in the full-blown Scottish version, and Ken participated exactly as his role was directed by custom. I did not attend the funeral, but my friends who did were amazed that Ken clearly knew what the customs were and accepted them, apparently willingly. He did not wear a kilt at the funeral, but that was apparently his only concession to his previous position of rejecting his Scottish heritage. I am told that Ken held up well through the entire ceremony until the pipers began to play at the end. At the instant he heard that sound, so profoundly loved by his father, he lost all emotional control and had to be supported physically by family members. I felt badly that I could not be there for Ken and also felt, albeit selfishly, that I'd missed another opportunity to see a transformation attributed to the musical elixir.

It was two days after the funeral before I was able to connect with Ken. He told me he was going out to the cemetery to "take care of some unfinished business," and if I wanted to meet him there, we could talk. We set a time to meet, and he gave me directions to the site.

I got there early, unintentionally, but it was an experience I would not trade for very much. It so happened that the road to the gravesite traveled in an uphill arc above and around the site Ken had given me and as I rode along it, I looked down on the peaceful repose below. I saw a young man, dressed in full Scottish regalia, playing the bagpipes reasonably well, marching around and around the grave of his father. I pulled over immediately because I knew that I should not intrude on this business and that I was serendipitously fortunate to be able to see it. I do not know how or when Ken learned to play bagpipes, but I know enough about the difficulty in playing them to know that it would have taken him years. I did not know that he owned his clan's tartans and accouterments or that he was even aware of the full customs of his people. But here it all was, clear and complete. As I watched him march, tears streaming down his face, playing those pipes loudly with such fierce intensity, I knew I was again seeing the elixir in action. I consider the opportunity to observe it and feel a bit of it vicariously as some of the most fortunate experiences I have ever had. If you believe in the power of the elixir as I do, then you must also accept that Ken's father somehow understood the message from wherever you believe he was then. I believe it fully.

I am a member of a proud bunch of old swamp Yankees named Pike. This is not an especially sophisticated group of folks—and they don't pretend to be. They know what they're about, tell you when they think you are wrong, don't express much affection or emotion, and live a long time. The family history, which I researched several years ago, cites person after person who lived into their nineties, even when the average in America was far below what it is now. They are a tough, physical bunch who like a good fight, either verbal or physical, and if you won't fight with them, they'll fight with each other. They can stay mad at each other and at others who have committed some transgression against them for years, even lifetimes.

My father was the youngest of four brother and three sisters. They are all gone now, and like their ancestors, none of them went especially early. The four brothers were locally famous, having been renowned athletes in their high school years. As they grew older, it became apparent that they each expected themselves and the others to live forever. So when the first and then the second brother died, it was especially difficult for the surviving brothers. In this situation, the elixir worked sort of backward, breaking down physical strength and resolve to allow the necessary emotions related to grief to escape. The stimulus again was music. This is not a musical group of people to say the least. I think they have always been a little suspect of my musical interest and ability, probably blaming it on my mother's Irish heritage.

A tradition was established for the Pike siblings when their mother died, apparently prematurely. I know my father was still in his young teens when she went, and since he was her favorite, he took it very hard. He could still remember the details of her funeral despite the fact that those details were more than seventy years old when he told them to me. The distinguishing centerpiece of that funeral, which attracted so many people that it made the front page of the paper, was the singing of a hymn called "In the Garden." To my father's limited musical ear, it is the most beautiful music he had ever heard, and he believed that it is the sound that carried his mother to heaven. Who among us can argue?

Whenever any of the Pike siblings left this world, that hymn is sung—always as a solo sung by a good female vocalist, therefore not by a Pike. The effect of that sound on these strapping people with broad shoulders, straight backs, and stoic faces is nothing short of astounding. Generally, when they hear that song, they turn first into Jell-O—and then to mush. All the repressed and stored-up emotions of their lives come freely flowing out of them. They are but children again, moaning their grief to their mother, who is clearly among them within the notes of that hymn. I wish I had met her when she was alive because she alone knew the secret of reaching the soft insides of these guys, and I wish I knew how she did it. I have been to several funerals with my father and uncles for people whom they loved deeply; without the hymn, the emotions they feel are not demonstrated. There is no cure for them without the elixir.

So I continue to search for the elixir. My research has shown me that it is usually associated with sound and that the sound that causes it goes straight past consciousness to the most fundamental emotions of the brain. I have experienced it myself, often. It is always unexpected and always joyful. Yet it is sometimes equally disturbing, like finding out that there are whole powerful parts of our psyche about which we know nothing.

A couple of years back, I had the chance to travel with a friend to Dublin. Our employer had an office there, and we went to conduct a management-training program. I was delighted to go to Ireland. My own Irish heritage is a relatively new area of exploration for me. For most of my life while my father was alive, I was taught that I am English and maybe a little Mohawk Indian. It was acknowledged that my mother was "pure" Irish, but that information was usually accompanied with derision or ugly humor. I know that she never protested this treatment, but later in her life, I began to get the picture at how much it hurt her, especially from the hands of the Pikes. Once I got the bigger context of my heritage I learned that I am far more Irish than anything else. Both my mother's parents were born in Ireland. Sadly, I do not know where or any of the other details of their pilgrimage to America.

While we were there, Gordon suggested that we take a historic bus tour of the city. I loved every minute of it. I began to feel strong emotional connections with the people and culture of Ireland. He took me to dinner at Temple Bar, a famous restaurant in Dublin whose history predates almost all of America's. Temple Bar has several floors of dining and drinking arrangements. After our dinner, we moved upstairs to the pub where a local Irish band was playing. I must admit that I was woefully ignorant of native Irish music, having only been exposed to the commercialized version sold here for Saint Patrick's Day celebrations.

I guess I shouldn't have been surprised at the impact of that music on me. But I was. In fact, I have never felt any music so deeply inside of me before. I knew instantly that this sound was a part of my DNA, and I was shocked to realize it. I thought of Tofie and more fully understood the joy of the elixir. I know that I alarmed Gordon a little because I was unable (actually unwilling) to converse with him while that music was being produced right in front of me. I was struck by the fact that three of the musicians were my age and two were just teenagers. The idea of teenagers learning and performing the ancestral music of their homeland was foreign to me. I realized that what I was seeing and hearing was a process that had been repeated for hundreds of years, like the stories of Native Americans told over and over again to the youth of the tribe to be certain that they would understand their own paths through life. I cannot fully capture the impact on me, but it remains with me strongly now and hopefully will for the rest of my life.

I believe that the more we can hear the sounds of life around us as music, the wider is the pathway by which the elixir can help us. The older I get, the more ways I find to provide access to it. We are becoming friends, the elixir and I, and I am eager to continue to develop our relationship.

An Abundance of Riches
2014

Every now and then, it is good for us to hop off the treadmill of our hectic lives and review where we are and where we've come from. Sometimes we confusedly think that running on the treadmill accounts for where we are and how we got there. But when we take the time for quiet reflection, when we reconnect with who we really are, we can be overwhelmed with an abundance of riches.

Such was my experience at the Camp Mohawk reunion last night. Working on camp issues has been the core of my volunteer life for many years, but the experience last night had little to do with worrying about enrollment, septic systems, or finances. No, last night was purely, joyfully, deliriously all about what camp means to so many people, what those people mean to each other, and what we have learned from each other. It was clearly and simply about an abundance of riches.

There are so many wonderful stories, so many wonderful memories, and so much catching up to do. As it always happens, no matter how long camp people have been away from each other and the camp itself, it takes but a few minutes to fully reconnect and regain those deeply powerful relationships we created as children. So the catching up part wasn't really our focus last night. Reconnecting was.

As I sat in the dining hall, looking at the faces, old and young, hearing the songs, singing the ones I knew, laughing at the old stories, and feeling the Mohawk spirit, my joy was nearly overwhelming. The spirit flows from us, to us, all around us, wrapping us safely in the security of knowing we are where we should be, with the people who still matter fifty years later (at least for me!). We take sustenance from it—and we contribute to it—in a perfect balance of giving and receiving. Who else could be provided with a greater abundance of riches?

As we talk and sing and laugh together, if we really pay attention, we find that ultimately we return to ourselves. We see the connection between our earliest development and what we are now. We see how much of what we offer to the world and what we take from it began in this place all those years ago. We are not surprised by it; we are validated. Who else gets to return to the place where they were free as children to discover their own strengths and weaknesses? Who else gets to return to the core of their own values system and then gets to share that experience with those who were there with them at the beginning, while it was forming? Who else gets to sit surrounded by love and an abundance of riches?

So many circles were connected last night that I did not know were still open—far too many to describe here. But just two will illustrate the connection of circles. I got to hug Ricky, who has the first emotionally and developmentally challenged camper to attend boy's camp. I was selected to be his counselor, and I was terrified at the prospect. Now I know that it was I who learned from Ricky—far more than he learned from me. We talked last night about those days all those years ago and were transported right back into them. We were both gloriously happy to be there.

At dinner, I got to talk with Tom Moore, my first real mentor. I thanked him for all that he means to me, and he explained that he always knew I would be up to whatever task he gave me. He told me why he chose me to be Ricky's counselor nearly forty years ago: he knew my potential even when I did not. The positive outcomes for everyone, flowing from Tom's faith in me through Ricky's amazing personality, just add to the abundance of riches.

So we packed up our sleeping bags, shed a tear or two at departing the place and people, and began looking forward to our next chance to go back to Mohawk—just as we did when we were kids. What we take away with us is renewal and reminders of who we are, what we can do, and the certain knowledge that we will bring to our worlds an abundance of riches.

SPIRIT
2011

I was recently involved in a discussion with an international team of trainers, consultants, philosophers, and friends. I have been a member of this team for nearly two years. The single source of our connection is the work of John Scherer, who also serves as my life coach and mentor. The topic of this discussion was a question about whether or not there is a spiritual epiphany requirement in the delivery of John's program: The Five Questions. As always, the discussion was lively and enlightening. For me, the discussion really transcended whether or not something spiritual was "supposed to happen" in a 5Q session. For me, the issue was more like about how we know when our spirits are fully engaged and growing.

Anyone who is even a bit introspective will say, "I know it when I see it or feel it." There is a sort of undeniable truth to that response. I listened to my associates try to describe what it meant for them to be "spiritual," and I realized that I've been trying to identify this phenomenon for a long time without actually consciously stating it.

As is often the case when I am working with this team, major parts of this "search" got clarified today. I want to capture them before they float away into the amorphousness of my nonconscious.

Steve said that he can get in touch with his own spirituality simply by viewing nature or artistic beauty. Dom said that he gets there when he loses awareness of himself. I was transported to what I experienced when I was a participant in the predecessor of the 5Q program back in 2003. We were in the process of a guided-imagery journey led by John. He asked us to go back into our lives and find the first time we could remember being in exactly the right place for us, of being completely free to be whoever we really are, and knowing that we were safe to be there. Instantly I was a kid of twelve or thirteen at Camp Mohawk, alone, watching the clouds on my back from the tall grass next to the soccer field. As I was transported to that joyful place, I could feel the grass, smell the marsh, and breathe the clean and purifying air. I was totally on my own at that moment, and it felt like the exact place I should be. I had all the rights and privileges of being in that place, and I was fully worthy of them. John described it as a polarity: being fully aware of yourself while simultaneously being beyond any sense of self.

When you drive into the main entrance of Camp Mohawk today, a large wooden sign welcomes you. The script at the bottom of the sign includes our motto: "Where the spirit lasts a lifetime." It has always resonated with me, and today I began to understand why even more than I had in the past. As a boy of thirteen, if you told me that you were developing my spirituality, I'd have been instantly resistant. That would have been translated into something religious, and by that age, I'd already had just about as much religion as I could stand—and none of it was positive. But the experience I had in camp was spiritual, powerful, and lifelong.

I tried to explain it several years ago to my fishing partners because it had become so strong a force within me that I could not continue to deny to them that I felt it. Of course they used it as a chance for ridicule as I expected them to, both suggesting that I had become a Bible-thumping evangelist and saying that I'd better not pull any of that crap on them. I remember that my reply to that attack was effective enough to stop it and end the discussion. The fact that it has never come up again as a source of teasing or ridicule leads me to believe that I may have hit something that resonated with them too, but they would never admit it. I said, "Nope. It has nothing to do with religion. It just seems to me that there is more to mankind than just mind and body, and if there is, I have as great an obligation to learn about it and develop it as I do with my mind and body."

So maybe the journey began on that day in camp. I was in complete control of who and what I am. The power and joy of simply being me—without a need for identity or approval—is a rare and often elusive experience. I love where the journey has taken me so far, and I expect it to never end.

CYNTHIA
JUNE 1994

For those of you who think words like *chum, pal, acquaintance,* or *buddy* are synonymous with the word *friend,* this piece probably won't make much sense to you. For those of you who understand the full potential and depth of the word *friend,* this might make sense on a fundamentally profound level.

We met three and a half years ago when Cynthia joined the corporate education department as a trainer and management consultant. I was already well acquainted with corporate education, working there as an independent adjunct instructor. Six months later, I joined the department as an associate of Cynthia's.

I guess our relationship began professionally. It only took about ten seconds for me to see she was a woman I could train with. I had (and still have) a reputation for being too stylistically strong to train with anyone else, and I would not argue the point. But when Cyn and I worked together in the front of the room, I realized that she had found a big, comfortable space that I was not in or planning to be in both physically and intellectually, and I was delighted to be up there with her. That feeling that we could each be ourselves completely, not behaviorally alike, but chasing identical goals, was a joy for me to experience. In a sense, it was a symbol for what our friendship was to become. In the most basic ways, we both knew it then and there in that classroom. I am sure it was invisible to the audience; we looked smooth and coordinated certainly, which would have been enough for them.

Three years ago, I would have spent lots of time trying to answer why we came into each other's lives when we did, but Cynthia has taught me that it is an unnecessary question. She believes that the universe is a series of alignments; sometimes you are aligned with them, and sometimes you are not. When you are, the thing to do is rejoice and use the energy to make progress. It is certain that you will not remain there indefinitely, and there is no point in trying to capture the moment forever. The key is to know yourself and those around you so that you can move on to the next alignment and learn the lesson that it brings to you.

For three years, we have watched the corporation cast suspicious eyes at our friendship. That we have been romantically linked is a matter of humorous indifference to us both because we know that most people are incapable of grasping what we are to each other. Simply stated, Cynthia is the only person I have ever known who sees every part of who I am—good, bad, or otherwise—and accepts the entire package without reservation. It has been a miracle of joy to find that I can do the same with her. Our primary level of communication is intuitive, and we can fully trust each other to be reliable on that level. It is not surprising that others assume that such a connection would include romance, yet in our case, it clearly does not.

I think it is significant that we became friends at highly volatile times in our lives. Cynthia would offer that as proof of a cosmic alignment, and I would not argue. We are almost the same age, and she alone seemed ready to help me through the difficult period of my midforties. Rather than prescribe for me or listen to my confusion and then offer solutions, Cynthia intuitively knows to let me talk. She challenges me to be clear— or to realize that I am not clear if an idea isn't ready yet. She knows that I deal with internal turmoil by talking about it and that just because I talk about it doesn't mean that I expect the listener to solve the puzzle.

I wish I could say I have listened to her as much as she does to me, but honesty prevents the attestation. In fact, it has been a source of tense moments between us that sometimes when she needs me most, I can only think about myself. I am learning to try harder to get out of my own way and allow room for her thoughts and concerns because they are important to me. For maybe the first time in my life, I am willing to break my own natural patterns of behavior simply because her friendship requires it.

Once I was really able to tune in to her heart, I found an intensely complex and powerful woman. She has taught me a great deal about the female psyche because she is willing to show it all to me: the good, bad, ugly, and very, very beautiful. The result is a friendship unlike any other I have ever known. It is one of those relationships that will last for life regardless of circumstances. I have only one other friendship even close to this one; even though Andy lives a thousand miles away, our friendship has not diminished. I am sure that Cynthia and I would be in the same boat.

JULIE

In June 1978, I left my job as assistant physical director at the Torrington Area YMCA and took a job in manufacturing. My motives were simple and straightforward. I had decided to pursue a graduate degree in organizational/industrial psychology and needed tuition reimbursement. My Y director had refused to consider any assistance unless I was willing to study a subject "related to my work," and since I thought organizational psychology was the core of my work at the Y, the decision to leave was easy.

Added to the clarity of the vision of my educational pathway were two other profoundly motivating factors. First, I was about to begin a formal study of industrial psychology—and up to that point in my work life, I had absolutely no experience in, or knowledge of, industry. In fact, when the personnel director offered me a job as a buyer in the machine-building division, I said, "Sure. I'll take the job. What's a buyer?" To say I was green in the job redefines the concept of green.

The other factor, besides a quest for experience, was simple. The new job's salary was 30 percent higher than I was getting at the Y. Perhaps there's a lesson in that too. At the Y, I held the top ranking in the Y's national computer for credentials, experience, and performance in aquatics, my area of specialization. I was in charge of training all instructors for all of New England in addition to my full curriculum in my home pools in Torrington. I worked a minimum of fifty hours per week and handled the regional-training assignment on the weekends for no additional money. After three years of that schedule, I was making $9,300 per year. If you are thinking it was a long time ago, gas and oil prices were out of sight in 1978. To go to a manufacturing job at over twelve thousand per year, have no duties after four thirty in the afternoon, and never work a weekend, I thought I'd gone to heaven.

From the moment I joined the Torin Corporation's machine division, my life was different. I was ready to move forward with my educational plans, and my desire for growth of all kinds was nearly obsessive. I had convinced them to hire me, not for what I knew about manufacturing (which was zero), but for how quickly I could learn. Now that boast was about to be put to the test. Somehow I survived and began to figure out what I was supposed to do. Some other time I will create the story about the "management" lessons I received from my first boss at Torin, but for now, suffice it to say that solid training skills were not in his arsenal. I began to pay as much attention as I could to who knew what, who made things happen, and how they did it.

At the end of one year, my boss left the company. I got his job. I knew I wasn't really ready for it—and so did my new boss—but he said he was sure I'd learn my way into it. I did. One of my first campaigns as purchasing agent was to get our purchasing clerk the attention and elevation she deserved. I knew how much of my survival was in her hands, and she was a fantastic performer. From that point, this story and its lessons really being.

I assumed that Julie viewed issues of "upward mobility" and gender equality with the same commitment and fervor that I did. I assumed she was interested in women's issues because every other woman I knew was. Back at the YMCA, women's issues were constant bones of contention, and I brought all those assumptions to my new job.

One of the primary parts of Julie's job was the manual typing and mailing of purchase orders. It may sound simple— and it often was—but the orders could get pretty complex. A simple omission, typo, or misunderstanding could cost the company significant amounts of money and trouble. The orders often included blueprints that detailed exactly what the vendors should provide. Therefore, when our engineering department offered a free, beginner-level course in blueprint reading (on company time), it made good sense to enroll Julie and attend myself. I had already arranged for tutoring the year before and felt relatively comfortable with it.

Frankly, as a secondary motivation in enrolling Julie, I was thinking about the implied status she would have if the company knew she could read blueprints, a skill not readily available among the clerical staff. I assumed that she shared my desire to elevate her status. After all, I was sure that all high performers wanted recognition for their contributions. I did, and I was sure that she did. Her response to my suggestion that she come with me to the class remains for me as one of the clearest lessons about managerial assumptions I have ever received. The gist of our conversation went like this:

"Engineering is offering a blueprint reading class. I'd like you to attend."

"Are you requiring it as a part of my job?" she asked quickly.

I did not expect nor was I prepared for this reaction.

"No, it isn't required as a part of your job. But it will make your job a bit easier, improve your performance overall, and increase the chances for promotion or more money," I replied.

"Are you saying that if I go to this class, I'll get raise? And if so, how much?" she asked even quicker.

"No, I'm not guaranteeing anything here at all. I just thought the idea would be appealing to you."

I was confused and defeated. Apparently it showed in my face.

She said, "Look, I've broken in three bosses before you. So let me help you clear up something about bosses right now. I realize that you are having a 'career,' and I'll do whatever I can to help you with it. I, on the other hand, am not having a 'career.' I have a job. It is not my life in any way. It is merely the means by which I have the money to afford my life, which I view as a series of events outside this place. I know you like my work—and I'm glad you do—but that's not why I do it. I work the way I do because it is the way I am. If I stay very busy all day long, then I don't dwell on this place or its people. So unless you tell me I must complete blueprint reading to keep my job, I'd rather just not be bothered. I might be bothered if a raise was substantial and guaranteed because that is what I come to work for, okay?"

I was shocked and angry with her for delivering this little lesson, but once I calmed down, I was able to separate my assumptions from Julie's brand of motivation. First, I thought about her lousy work attitude. Then I looked at her performance, which was clearly well beyond the requirements of the job and clearly superior to others at the same level. According to all I ever believed previously about motivation, she could not possibly feel this way and do good work, yet by all the standards I— and the company—had to measure performance, her work was excellent.

I began to realize a vital lesson about how people approach work. More importantly, I began to realize that everyone didn't have to think like me to perform well. In fact, as I learned more about motivation in graduate school over the next several months, I learned that a manager's work attitudes are often the exception within the workplace, not the rule. Rewards are often designed in accordance with the values of the manager granting them—rather than from the value system of those receiving them. As such, the receivers often don't view them as rewards at all.

Perhaps this lesson seems trite and obvious, but for me, it was a thunderbolt of illumination. So many other issues related to motivation and attitude on the job became clearer. Julie and I are still friends today, perhaps because we exchanged viewpoints regularly throughout our tenure of working together. We did not always agree, but I really enjoyed the dialogue. She told me later that I was the first manager who simply talked to her and allowed her to disagree. When we began, she couldn't disagree without anger, but we worked on that. Perhaps that's where our friendship began. Like so many of the lasting friendships I have had from my work experience, this one began with a lesson in working together—and it remains as valuable now as the day I got it.

JOSE:
A SHORT-LADLE POURER

Years ago, when I was a young, eager, independent training consultant, one of my clients had a foundry. Foundries generally are not especially renowned for progressive management. Their world is one of difficult work environments (the temperature on the floor of the foundry during the "pour" is often above 120 degrees), and typically their hourly workforce is not especially formally educated or sophisticated. That is not to say that those men and women aren't skilled and highly motivated. In the foundry where I was working with the supervisors, the workforce was devoted to and intensely proud of their work. Their turnover was not high, and absenteeism was low. They were remarkably close to a self-managed workforce. Much of this was due to the highly effective leadership that ran the foundry, but the rest came from the pride of the workforce.

In this foundry, as in many across the country, the largest demographic within the workforce was Portuguese. The Portuguese consider themselves the world's foundry men, going back as long as there have been foundries. They are a hardworking, dedicated, and intensely proud lot. I learned to respect them in my work with the foundry supervisors (some of whom were also Portuguese).

Early on, the guys told me about Jose. He was noteworthy on a number of fronts—not the least of which was never having missed a day of work in forty-two years. I was skeptical, but the records confirmed the claim. He had not missed a single day of work for longer than I had been alive. It was a remarkable achievement, yet among this population, it was not especially noteworthy. "Sure," they said, "he had a long record going, but it was what we should expect from guys like Jose." I was amazed.

My amazement only increased when I found out what he actually did in the foundry. When castings are made in a gray or ductile iron foundry, it is the result of enormous cauldrons of molten metal carried overhead on an elaborate crane and conveyor system to sites on the pouring floor. The cauldron would tip and pour its volcanic contents into molds, amid a shower of sparks and escaping gases. After the pour, the castings would "vent" as they cooled, releasing their pent-up gases in the form of flames periodically shooting from the mold as it sat on the sandy foundry floor. Not a friendly place to be if you didn't have the ear and savvy to know when such a venting might happen. When I asked about injuries and first-aid training for the employees in a different foundry, the plant manager said, "Well, we don't get as many injuries as you might expect. Our bigger problem is fatalities."

The castings that were too small to be able to be poured directly from the "pot" were poured by hand. A long-handled smaller pot was placed on the floor and filled from the overhead pot. A man would lift that heavy pot quickly and efficiently and pour the contents into the smaller molds. That put him right down on the pouring floor during the pour—in an environment so hostile that very few men or women could tolerate it. For the sake of this story, let's call that job "short-ladle pourer," and only two or three employees had the skill and tenacity to handle the assignment. One of those people was Jose.

The rest of the workforce typically thought the short-ladle pourers were crazy. It took a special kind of person to do that work, so I was very interested in talking to Jose about his view of his work. When I asked for permission to approach him, I was told that he would not talk to me. It wasn't just me. Jose was labeled as a sociopath. He had no friends at work, no social life that anyone knew about, no family, and no outside interests—all the more reason why I needed to talk to him.

For several days, I waited in the cafeteria for him to come in for his morning break. The first day I met him at the coffee machine and introduced myself. He completely ignored me except to glare at me in a menacing way. When he approached the coffee machine the next day, I put the money in and told him it was on me. He glared again, but he accepted the coffee without a word. This continued for several days until he stopped at the machine and said, "What do you want? Why are you doing this? Leave me alone."

I answered, "All I want is five or ten minutes of your time to talk."

He said, "If I talk to you for five minutes today, will you go away and leave me alone after that?"

I assured him that I would, and he agreed to talk. I said, "So, Jose, how is it possible that a guy could do what you do for so long? You've been doing it for longer than I have been alive, and the work is surely not easy. How do you do it?"

After a long pause, punctuated by a disgusted glare on his face, he replied, "All you punks think I am just a short-ladle pourer!"

"Well, aren't you?" I replied.

"That's just my job title. What I think I do is pour the foundation for American industry. What I am making is necessary to keep the wheels of industry rolling. It's very important that I do it correctly and consistently. Nobody else does it better than me because that is what the work demands. It has to happen on time and every day, and it has to be right. I consider it an honor to be able to do it."

All these years later, Jose has no idea what a lesson he taught me that day. It was something I had already known, but it was buried in my brain because it was a bit altruistic, as opposed to the science and hard logic that I had been trained to believe in.

Jose was more real than statistics, projections, theories, or models. He has always been my go-to home base for understanding anyone's work. I often hear Jose's voice murmuring behind my own as I express my own GPS (greater purpose statement): A formidable force, an avid developer of the possible human, infused, I unlock doors and set people aflight on their own pathway. As I trust the unfolding of my gifts, I know my place and rejoice.

Thanks, Jose. I am happy to have met you, and since then, I have been looking for others who get it the way you and I do.

THE PATHWAY

I was describing to a friend recently that for some time now I have felt off balance. Since she is a trained listener and knows that I seek better understanding of myself, she asked me to describe what it means and feels like to be "off balance." Right off the top of my head, I found that I could do it, at least well enough for her to grasp some of what I was feeling.

The Native American concept of the "pathway" is the best example of what I seek to do with my life. It is defined as a narrow pathway upon which one strives to travel toward whatever mission the Great Spirit has given us. For me, the idea is best described in Abraham Maslow's idea of self-actualization, the highest of human needs. I do not know what will happen to me ahead on the pathway, but I know it contains some element of the total person I can become. I know that each step along it is preparation for each next step. I also know that traveling the pathway feels like heaven on earth—and maybe it is.

The feeling of serenity, quiet joy, and total confidence that I am where I am supposed to be when I am on it inspires me and draws me more powerfully than anything I have ever experienced.

I know that remaining "on balance" on this narrow pathway is very, very difficult and sometimes feels almost impossible. That's because the environment on either side of the pathway is often enticing, compelling, seductive, and powerful. I know I will leave the pathway for periods of time, sometimes of necessity, sometimes because of making wrong decisions. The times I must leave it of necessity are often associated with the world of making a living or being reliable to others in some specific way. I believe that I can become ill only when I am not on the pathway and know I cannot return to it while I am ill.

My friend asked me to describe myself when I am on the pathway. I found that I could easily picture myself as I walk the pathway. I am not as tall, because I have no need to stand rigidly or hold my body in "ready" mode. Also, I am softer and rounder— like when we learn to fully relax our muscles. Functional, but not alarmed, I am often silent as I walk since I do not need to seek information or tell it to others. My mind contains no questions or answers, because I know that all I need is within me if I am silent and listen. I am never fatigued, worried, or hurried. I do not need to evaluate myself or solicit evaluations from others. That I am on the pathway is all the feedback I need.

It almost always makes more sense to understand human behavior as a point on a continuum of choices. I realize I can still feel relatively balanced if I am off the pathway but still near enough to it to see direction, especially if I have left it of my own volition. To know that I have intentionally moved off the center of the path in pursuit of some value feels fine with two qualifiers: the time needed to stray must be of short and known duration and if the distance from the center of the pathway is not so far away that I lose sight of its directive force in my life.

I was not surprised when my friend asked me to describe myself when I am too far off the pathway for whatever reason. I was prepared for this question. I realized that the answer wasn't simply the opposite of the description above; instead, it had a set of defined behaviors that made me realize I'd spent more time off the pathway than I'd wanted to. Much of my behavior would seem consistent to anyone walking through rough terrain without a pathway. Clumsy, crashing behavior. Discovery of things by sheer accident rather than destiny. Fatigued all the time because of extra energy needed to cover the difficult ground. Quickly impatient, angry, emotionally volatile. I would also be competitive and physically dominant. I would likely be effective in my endeavors off the pathway, surviving on a strong will, a powerful desire to never quit, a relatively flexible intellect, and strong problem-solving skills. The rewards and benefits that might come to me through these behaviors would provide satisfaction—but only for a very short time. In fact, I would often be unhappy with the reward's size and volume largely because it did not make me feel as good as I felt walking the pathway. That others might like me or praise me for my performance off the pathway would only add to my sense of guilt and sorrow. To become really good at a job off the pathway is a dangerous reality within my life. It is seductive to my own insecurities since those around me who do not understand or endorse the pathway have little patience with any dissatisfaction I might express while I am successful at the wrong tasks.

My first discovery of being "good at a thing I hate" happened when I left my job as a YMCA aquatics director (a job I truly loved) and went to work in manufacturing. I knew that I wanted to get a master's degree in organizational psychology, and the Y was not interested in providing tuition reimbursement. Instead, I became a buyer for a company that made machines that made springs.

I was appalled that people could work in such a non-people-friendly environment. It was a world of numbers, record keeping, political infighting, and power struggles. Once I learned how the system worked and what was expected of me, I did really well in my job—even though I thought the whole idea was destructive to people. My boss quit after my first year, and I got his job as purchasing agent. I expanded the function within purchasing and found ways to save the company lots of money. I attended graduate school at night and did all my graduate research in our factory. Within three years, I'd gotten several raises and promotions and was making five times what I'd earned at the Y. I had job offers in purchasing from several headhunters and was tempted by each because the money was attractive.

But I hated getting up each day and going there. I'd been able to buy a home in Litchfield as a result of my success there, made lifelong friends there, and was still very successful and respected within the company and among my vendors. In my mind, I was nothing but a two-bit sellout. That I could be so successful in an environment that viewed employees as liabilities made me feel like a hooker. The more ruthlessly aggressive I became, the more everybody around me liked it.

My efforts to talk with the important people in my life about these feelings were unsuccessful and added to the negative feelings. My wife suggested that I needed to accept the fact that the world is a cold, heartless place. She thought my expectations were too high and I should just take the money and shut up. Even my parents told me that the world they grew up in dictated that if you had a good job, you kept it—and you thwarted anyone who threatened your job or security.

The concept of the pathway was not clearly defined at that point in my life, but I knew that my misery with success at a job I hated was too strong to ignore. When I finished graduate school and the manufacturing company began to fail, I left and began my own training company, offering sales training to the companies that had previously been my vendors. Conceptually, I remained in the brambles off the pathway, but I moved close enough to it to at least feel its direction.

In hindsight, the decision to leave that world of success and reliability and strike out on my own was really the beginning of the end of my first marriage. From her point of view, I had turned my back on my wife and children to go tilting at windmills and "what might be." I was unable to adequately explain it—probably because I did not understand it very well myself. Since then, I have done it again twice more by accepting jobs with lots of monetary rewards in environments I hated. Within those two scenarios, I began to understand who I really was and what the pathway meant.

I am now working much closer to the pathway. I am married to woman who "gets it" conceptually and who seeks her own pathway as well. The unstable nature of independent training and consulting still keeps me up at night, but so far, I have been able to withstand the uncertainty of my profession and give in to the temptation to get "a real job" with benefits and big money, working somewhere I'd hate.

THIS PLACE DOESN'T MATTER

Compared to the real joys in life,
this place doesn't matter.
Compared to the laughter of a happy child,
this place doesn't matter.
Compared to a vermillion sunrise,
this place doesn't matter.
Compared to the joy of feeling well again after illness,
this place doesn't matter.
Compared to the life in the eyes of a grandfather
while he dances with his granddaughter,
this place doesn't matter.
Compared to the endless, bottomless,
unqualified miracle of simply being loved,
this place doesn't matter.
Compared to knowing that you have tried hard,
lived honestly, and been true to yourself,
this place doesn't matter.
Compared to all the other places you've been
when you found any of the real joys of life,
this place doesn't matter.
Compared to the astounding tidal wave of power
from people working and being together,
this place doesn't matter.
If we have any mission at all, it must be to try
to find those things that really do matter,
and only if and when we find them here
will this place ever matter.

ACKNOWLEDGEMENTS

There are several people who I wish to thank for their roles in the creation of this book:

First of all to everyone who has read these pieces, one piece at a time and encouraged me to publish them, thank you for your pushing, nudging and thoroughly appreciated encouragement.

To Kathy Davis, this just might be what I haven't "let on" the world to see. Thanks for your coaching.

To John Scherer, whose guidance helped me set a new direction in my life, which includes this book.

To Lois, my partner in life, always in my corner, always my voice of encouragement, my perpetual love.

Lastly to Karen Moulton, whose keyboard, organizational and formatting skills turned the original pile of stories into a manuscript; but even more who has a been a constant voice of support and encouragement for my writing, my heartfelt gratitude.